THE TOR KING

by
R. S. Barrett

Paperback Edition
ISBN: 978-0-9908833-0-2

Published by:
    1st Class Document Services
    Winston-Salem, NC
        1stclassdocumentservices.com

Cover photo: Sunset at Glastonbury Tor
by Matthew Collingwood
Photo obtained through www.canstockphoto.com
License agreement 0145410

TABLE OF CONTENTS

PROLOGUE

There are many mysterious places to ignite the fire of imagination, but few perhaps that harbor so much history and lore as the Glastonbury Tor of England. Was Saint Collin really taken to a castle below the Tor by Gwyn ap Nudd, King of the Fairies, ruler of the Netherworld, exorcising his escape by the sprinkling of holy water? Or, is it just folklore? They say strange things still occur on the Tor, in the mists of Avalon.

THE TOR KING

THE MISTS OF AVALON

A sudden blast of wind swept over the lowland lifting a dry colorless leaf, wafting it upward against a backdrop of mountainous green, the Glastonbury Tor, which stood like a beacon against the surrounding lowland.

Aslinn smiled, then reached up and kissed him. She ran her fingers through Dale's thick dark hair.

"You've got the gift of storytelling, Dale Conklin, same as your mum."

"You're the one gift I never want to be without, Aslinn."

She narrowed her eyes, "I'm not a gift." She started backwards up the slope of the Tor. "And my affections are not cheap either."

Dale started toward her, but she put up her hand and stuck her chin out. "But --", she smiled, "if you can catch me, you may give me a kiss." Aslinn's long blonde hair swirled around her as she turned abruptly and ran swiftly up the slope, the lilt of her laughter carried in the cooling early evening air.

Dale bolted after her. He was upon her in seconds. His arm reached around her waist and pulled her in, then down. They fell into the ivy beside the sloping path. She was still laughing, but Dale was consumed with jealous thoughts and anxious desire to be her one and only. He took his kiss with the warmth of her body pressed lightly against him then pushed himself on top of her and his kiss became stronger, deeper. All his desire, mixed with fear of losing her, made his passion grow stronger, hotter.

At first she gave him slight resistance, but then she quickly gave in to the passion too and Dale moved his lips to her ears and neck. Her perfume mingled with the sweet fragrance of earth and ivy.

"Ow..."

Dale snapped out of his daze and lifted himself off of her to see the cause of her discomfort.

Aslinn began pulling her long hair from the brush that it had become tangled in and Dale rolled over beside her. His foot wrapped in the ivy as he did, but he didn't notice it. He helped pull her long strands loose as she sat up then watched Aslinn comb her fingers through the soft tresses to set them straight again. His face was set in stern concentration and Aslinn noticed this.

"What's wrong?"

"Nothing," he lied.

She brushed her dress with her hands, "You sure, you've been acting funny all afternoon."

Dale bit his lip. His eyes searched the lowering sun in the sky. He could feel the moisture in the air. It would likely bring a fog tonight, but his thoughts were not on the weather, instead his mind raced back to the events that had been haunting him since the end of day in school when he saw Aslinn in Mr. Ayer's physics lab and watched silently as Ian McBride kissed her.

Dale shuddered with a chill, uncertain if it came from his thoughts or the cooling evening air. "I saw you kissing Ian today." He turned his gaze to her and was surprised by what he saw. Aslinn smirked. She actually seemed pleased. Dale felt suddenly confused with a mix of both anger and hurt he didn't know how to react. He was afraid to be angry with her. Afraid that that was all she would need to break it off with him and have her excuse to go to Ian.

Aslinn cocked her head, "And you didn't say anything all this time? What took so long?" Dale stared. Still unsure how best to respond and almost wishing he had said nothing at all, but what was the reason behind the mischievous glint in her pale blue eyes.

"Are you jealous?"

"You're my girl!"

"I didn't kiss him, he kissed me."

"You didn't seem to mind it much." The ire was beginning to put heat back into his cool limbs. Dale scrambled to his feet, tearing the ivy from the ground, leaving a small wreath of it wrapped around his ankle that was quickly concealed beneath his pants leg. Aslinn stood too and gazed into his dark, glaring eyes. Then she moved toward him.

Dale stood perfectly still, his eyes burning on her soft, pale skin. She reached her right hand behind his neck and with her left hand over his shoulder she smiled coyly before pulling herself up to kiss him. Dale pulled away from her. How could he let her treat him this way? And why would she want to if she truly loved him, as she said she did? Dale knew Aslinn was fully aware of her beauty and that she enjoyed the attention it brought her. Did he really possess her love? Was their relationship just a small town romance born out small town choices that she would quickly outgrow with big city opportunity? They had been going steady since they were fourteen. Now, in their last year of school, what might happen with Aslinn set to go away to university where they would be separated for the first time? The chill ran through him again as he stared at her with an ache in his heart that nearly tore him apart.

Aslinn reached up, stroking his face with the back of her hand. She smiled, "I'm glad you're jealous. Show's you care." Then he let her hand move back around his neck and she reached up again. This time he let her kiss him, but it was not as he expected. Her kiss was forceful and the heat of their earlier passion began to rise up in him again.

Dale wrapped his arms around Aslinn holding her tight against him. He gave back the kiss as strongly as before feeling her come back to him with the answer he desired, or the fear he chose to deny. When they stood apart Aslinn was smiling sweetly and Dale let himself be sated in the knowledge that she was still his. That Aslinn did love him, as he loved her. This was forever. This was always. And he wouldn't let his mind accept it any other way.

Dale glanced around. "Have you noticed we're the only two up here this evening?"

"Well of course my lord, I decreed it to be so. All of our subjects are to refrain from coming upon the Tor this evening so that the king and I shall be able to survey our kingdom without distraction."

It was the game they'd played since they were children. They were like Arthur and Guinevere on

Avalon and it had begun on the day when they first met. Aslinn was there with her parents and her younger sister, Beth. They had been running through and around the tower on the Tor's pinnacle playing tag and when they had exhausted themselves and sat down to catch their breathes, the girls began to slip into their regal roles as princesses. Dale was not to be left out, of course, and so he declared himself as king. Then Aslinn insisted, if Dale was going to be king that she should be queen. And so it had always been from that day on.

There had been many times over the years when the three of them would go to the Tor to play their game. Then there was that day when Beth had been sick with a cold and hadn't gone with them. That was the first time Dale had kissed Aslinn, in the tower, when a soft warm breeze had floated a strand of hair down her cheek.

Dale remembered it as if it were yesterday. It was not long after Aslinn's twelfth birthday. He had scraped his knuckles in a fall from his bike earlier in the day. The bandage had worked loose and Aslinn was holding his hand while gingerly trying to reattach it. She had grimaced at the thought of how painful it must be when she saw the scraped raw skin and that touched him. Then the breeze wafted the hair around her face. And he kissed her. Their first kiss.

Dale gazed at Aslinn now. The twilight glowed around her like an aura and he felt a prick, a painful stab to his heart, at the thought that she should ever give her affections to another. It wasn't just Ian's kiss that brought this pain. Those dark thoughts stung him with increasing frequency as time brought the certainty of their eventual separation.

Her parents, though not rich, were much better able to provide for their children than his struggling widow mother could for him. Dale's clothes were clean and neat and that, his mother said, was what was important. Aslinn parents, however, proud of their beautiful child, never spared her the things that her heart desired. Aslinn was always impeccably dressed in the latest fashion from the best shops. She would go to university and Dale would likely go to work. He wondered, would those things she'd never been without ever mean more to her than he? If he could not provide them, would she always love him?

She stretched out her hand and he took it. "Let's go to the top and survey our kingdom, my lord."

"All right", he smiled. "But it's getting late and I'm getting hungry."

She smiled and pulled him along until they were again walking up the gentle slope. A mist was beginning to form and move up the Tor behind them.

Dale released all his insecurities and let the usual, comfortable happiness overtake him, "Let's go to King's for dinner. We can take some sausages back for Beth."

Dim lights glowed along the path and became brighter as the sun set deeper in the sky.

"You spoil her because you know she's got a crush on you."

"She's just a kiddie, Aslinn."

Aslinn glanced at Dale. "Even kiddies know what love is. Love is something that grows up with you."

Dale gazed at Aslinn and thought about what she said. His love for her had certainly grown over the years, then Aslinn stopped abruptly and stared up the path.

"Look, Dale. Look at how the path glows." She shuddered and grabbed Dale's arm tightly. Her voice was a whisper, "It's the work of the fairy king."

Dale shot her a glance of scorn, but Aslinn didn't notice it, she was still fixed on the eerie glow before them. Their steps had slowed, but they continued upward and Dale had to admit to himself that it was indeed...strange. It must have something to do with the fog and a reflection of lights in the sky, but whatever it was he certainly couldn't give credence to Aslinn's explanation. "That's all nonsense, Aslinn."

Her voice was still a whisper, "But you know what they say. You know the stories better than anyone."

Dale wasn't going to let Aslinn's foolish fears pervade, in spite of the prickling hairs on his neck. "The devil with Gwyn ap Nudd," he said.

Then, in a breath of an instant, small blue lights swooped before them. They came so suddenly, that Dale couldn't say if they had come from the sky or the ground. They were just immediately there and they danced all around them in the backdrop of darkening sky.

Aslinn drew nearer to Dale and he held her tight as they both gazed startled at what they couldn't explain. They couldn't move in any direction that they were afraid they might run into the strange blue orbs and they watched as they swirled and moved in upon them, coming nearer.

Aslinn gasped, "Dale." It came out like a breath and he pulled Aslinn backwards against him. Dale wanted to run, but not wanting to take his eyes off the awesome encroaching lights, he just held there and watched, his eyes fixed in fascination. The hair on his neck and arms prickled and it was as if something inside him clicked on a switch of alarm. Dale took another step back, pulling Aslinn with him ready to turn and...*RUN!* His mind screamed it, but before he could say it or move they were surrounded in a swarm of little blue orbiting lights.

Dale stood frozen in trepidation. Then Aslinn stretched her hand out as if to touch one of the tiny lights with her finger. Dale reached to pull her hand back, but before she could reach it, it blended into another. And the two together became larger than each on its own.

Aslinn's hand snapped back and Dale grabbed it. Other orbs of light zipped into the larger one, each time growing larger until they had converged into one large ball of blue light that shone brightly before them. Dale tried to notice if he could see through the light, but it was bright, so very bright that he could see nothing beyond it and then it moved towards them. It moved upon them and they were enveloped in its bright blue haze.

The light was blinding and they put their hands up in front of their eyes to shield them from its brightness. Then the light began to slowly dim and when it had fully diminished, the world had changed.

Torch lights glowed brightly in their sconces along stone walls. Beautiful young women dressed in flowing blue and red silk gowns and handsome young men in silk and satin of the same colors were standing all around them.

"Dale! Where are we? What is this place?"

A movement caught in the corner of his eye and Dale turned toward it. Two stalwart soldiers with bared chest stood by steps that led to...a throne? From it, a tall handsome man Dale guessed to be of about the age of twenty-five, moved down the center of the steps toward him.

His appearance was regal beyond that of the gold crown encrusted in diamond, sapphire and ruby. His jeweled red satin shirt was trimmed in blue and stretched over his taut muscles. A red cape of matching colors draped over his broad shoulders and fell to just below the back of his knees. Trousers of blue satin were tucked into polished red boots that had the look of snake skin. Then Dale noticed his eyes. There was a darkness in them which caused a shiver to run down his spine and into the depths of his soul. The king, as obviously he was, held Aslinn's gaze with his own as he descended and came towards them.

When he stood close before them he finally let his gaze turn toward Dale and with a slight grin he said, "The devil with me, you said. Now the devil's with you."

Dale's body tingled in apprehension and he pulled Aslinn close against him, but she seemed not to feel the need of his protective grasp. There was no tension in her limbs as she stood smiling and staring at her handsome host, so brilliant in his colorful appearance. She was no longer afraid, but rather enthralled and excited by the mystical man.

He swept his hand around. "We have prepared a feast in your honor. For the king and..." he took her hand, "this most lovely queen of the Tor." He kissed her fingers lightly and Dale shook visibly from the anger that welled inside by Aslinn's obvious enjoyment of the gesture.

Abruptly Dale noticed an array of smells and as he glanced around he saw that there were tables lining the main hall laden with food of every kind: roasted pig, trays of fresh fruit, huge pots of stew, cakes and loaves of bread. The fresh baked aroma caused Dale's stomach to grumble and he realized again that he was hungry.

It was a sight such as neither one had seen before. The tables were set lavishly in gold and silver upon colorful silk linens.

It was indeed a royal feast, as one might have expected to see in King Arthur's court. But this was not Arthur's court Dale reminded himself.

Still he couldn't believe all of this was really happening - or was it real? It must be a dream. But then his senses went into full alarm as if breaking away from a spell in a moment that had turned into an hour. Dale reached for Aslinn's arm and pulled her back yelling, "No!"

But not even this turned Aslinn's attention away from her enthralling host and he kept his gaze upon her. They ignored him so completely that Dale wondered if he had not become invisible and he watched them intently and silently for a moment as if he were.

Aslinn positively gleamed at the king's beguiling attention. He gestured with his hand and musicians struck up their instruments and began to play a lively, light melody. He smiled at her adoringly and took her hand in his. Aslinn's eyes fluttered as she looked up at him shyly, "This is all for us?"

Then with a slight bow he replied, "But of course, my lady."

Dale was incensed. She obviously did know he was there and yet she took blatant pleasure in another man. Making matters worse was her insane naivety not to understand or care who he was. Frustrated, Dale screamed at her, "Aslinn!"

She turned her head slightly, finally acknowledging him and Dale couldn't believe the excitement he saw in her eyes.

"Just look at it all, Dale. Isn't it wonderful?"

Dale was aghast. *Wonderful!* How could she be so foolish? This was no childish game. They were in Annwn, in Gwyn ap Nudd's castle beneath the Tor. She herself had been the first to conjecture what was happening. How could she not understand that now?

Helplessly, he watched her let Gwyn lead her to a table leaving him standing there gaping in confused aggravation. There had to be a way to end this madness. With determination to make her see sense, Dale strode up behind Aslinn. He grabbed her arm, pulling her back again, but even with this rough behavior she didn't look at him. She continued to stare at Gwyn, unable to take her eyes off of him as if she were bewitched. And suddenly Dale knew it was so.

He pulled back on her again, "Aslinn, he's the devil. You can't give in to him."

But Aslinn stared out in awe, "Look, how lovely everything is. Isn't it just like we always dreamed it would be."

Dale's tone was low and serious, "This isn't a game, Aslinn." But feeling he couldn't convince Aslinn that it wasn't, the heavy lurch in the pit of his stomach made him wish that it were a game.

But again she ignored him. She was taken in by all the beauty that surrounded her…and Gwyn; and she smiled at him and took his proffered arm.

Fairies began to dance to the music and although the tune was light and whimsical the melodic notes were so heavy that Dale could feel them moving through him. Reluctantly he followed Aslinn to the table and took his seat beside her.

The rumbling in Dale's stomach grew stronger with the sight and smells of so much food within reach. But remembering the fairy stories his mother had told him as a child, because they were his favorites, he knew that he couldn't take even one bite, for just one taste could enslave him here forever.

Servants flowed about, poured drinks in silver goblets and set them down. Gwyn reached out for a tray of meats, cheeses and fruit. He pushed it toward Aslinn and Dale and Dale watched in horror as she picked food from it to fill her plate. Is she already so entranced that she can't understand what she's doing?

A beautiful servant woman moved between Dale and Aslinn offering the sweet smelling foods to Dale, but he pushed it and her away to set his eyes intently upon Aslinn and Gwyn. He could not let her out of his sight, lest she give in to Gwyn before they had their chance to escape and he began to look around for an obvious exit, but there was none.

Gwyn stared into Aslinn's eyes. He held her hand in his and Dale grew white hot with anger. Right in front of him she flirted with Gwyn as if she had no care of him. Suddenly "flirting with the devil" took on a more literal meaning and Dale shuddered with the thought. Is that what they had been doing when they pronounced themselves king and queen of the Tor?

Aslinn gazed upon the large stones set into the cloth of Gwyn's shirt. The large rubies and sapphires shimmered in the candlelight.

Gwyn noticed the glint in Aslinn's eyes as she stared at the jewels and he put his hands on his chest. "You fancy these bobbles?"

Aslinn eyes went wide, "Oh yes, they're beautiful. I've never seen anything like them."

Gwyn smiled at her then moving his hands across the jewels he pulled them away to produce a necklace on a gold chain with glittering diamonds filling the spaces between the jewels and he placed it around her neck.

Dale shoved the plate in front of Aslinn off the end of the table, spilling the food all over the floor at Gwyn's feet, breaking his mesmerizing hold on Aslinn. Gwyn looked at the food then lifted his dark gaze to Dale.

His eyes seemed to glow and it sent another shudder through Dale making his voice shake. "We don't want your food or your stuff. All we want is to go home. Tell us the way back, Gwyn ap Nudd."

Aslinn put her hand on Dale's arm, "Please Dale," then turned her gaze on Gwyn again, "not yet."

Gwyn grinned at her and she smiled back and he reached up to lift a strand of Aslinn's hair off her cheek and caressed it with his fingers. Then Gwyn turned his gaze back on Dale and though he still smiled Dale saw what was in his eyes and they were dark, hollow and empty.

"In good time lad...in time, but for now let us have fun and merriment. Eat, enjoy! This is all in your honor after all, young king." Then Gwyn took Aslinn's hand again and stood. "Shall we dance?" Aslinn stood to go with him.

Every nerve and muscle in Dale's body was screaming and he shouted after her, "Aslinn! Aslinn!"

But she threw her head back, swept her arm around and glancing at her surroundings said, "Everything is so beautiful. Why shouldn't we stay a while and have fun."

Dale flew hot with anger. It was obvious that Aslinn was not in her right mind. She was becoming entranced and he had to do something to break her trance. He pushed his chair back to go after her as she followed Gwyn into the mix of jubilant dancers.

Dale's mind went frantically searching all the fairy folklore he knew for something that would help. There was an answer in those stories that his mother had told him over and over again at his begging, but he seemed unable to focus. Was he becoming entranced too? Then he felt a light touch on his shoulder and Dale turned to see what it was.

She was beautiful. Her long red hair cascaded in waves over her shoulders and brushed his arm as she reached for his hand.

"My name is Gwyllion. Dance with me, my lord. Let us make merry."

Her silk gown in many layers of red and blue silk had a neatly tattered appearance that flowed from the high waist to cover her red satin shoes. He thought how she looked like a flame come to life and that thought brought him back to his plight, back to the realization that he was, as St. Collin once was, in the realm of the Netherworld.

"I don't want to dance."

She leaned down and whispered in his ear. "I will show the way out."

Dale was suspicious, but he allowed her to lead him to the dance. At least there he could keep a closer eye on Aslinn while he tried to think of a way to escape.

They moved through the throng of dancers and Dale's eye's searched for Aslinn and Gwyn among them. The music was haunting. The rhythm felt as if it flowed through him. *Gwyllion,* his mind searched her name among the lore, but he couldn't recall what he knew he should be able too. All he knew was what he felt and he put it into his mind over and over. *Don't trust Gwyllion...don't trust Gwyllion.*

She moved gracefully and drew close to Dale. He could feel her warmth, smell the sweet fragrance of laurel...*mountain goddess! That was it! She mislead travelers to meet their doom.* Then he heard Aslinn's laugher and his eyes followed the sound.

Aslinn's back was to him and Gwyn's smile, as she danced in his close embrace, made Dale seethe. He moved to go nearer, but Gwyllion raised one of the fine layers of her silk dress like a veil and swirled around him preventing his advance in the tight throng of dancers that suddenly seemed to grow tighter.

Gwyn moved Aslinn in their dance near to a table. He kept one arm wrapped around her waist while he reached for a goblet and took a drink.

"Hmm, the wine is sweet, but not so sweet as thee."

Aslinn gleamed with delight at his words and he twirled her into his arms then brought the goblet up to her mouth. "It would be sweeter still on your lips, my lady."

Gwyllion ceased her twirling to press close against Dale, but he moved away from her nearness and searched for Aslinn again not seeing her where he last had. Gwyllion laughed while she twirled about him and the thought occurred to Dale how happy he would be if it were Aslinn dancing with him that way. Then his eyes went to searching for her again. He knew she was falling under Gwyn's spell and he had to get them out before she tasted knowledge.

"You said you would show me the way out."

"You have only just arrived."

Dale grabbed her arm and glared angrily into her eyes. But she just laughed again then leaned in close. Her hand slipped behind his neck and Dale felt the tingle of her breath as she whispered in his ear.

"Through that hall." Dale turned to see where she was pointing. There were many halls that led out from the great room they were in. Gwyllion nibbled at his ear and Dale cringed involuntarily at the sensation and pulled away, but she pulled on his arm and drew herself close to whisper again.

"At the first passage turn right, go two more then right again and you will back on top of the Tor."

She wrapped her arms around him, but Dale wiggled out of her embrace. Undaunted, Gwyllion came close again. She ran her hands over his chest and shoulders then drew herself tight against him. "There is no need to hurry. There is much to enjoy here."

Dale stared into her eyes and it was as if staring into a deep dark well. He felt a sensation of falling and blinked to release himself from her gaze. He pulled her arms down and backed away then moved through the dancers toward Aslinn.

Aslinn was wrapped in Gwyn's arms her head upon his chest and couldn't see him approach her from behind, but Gwyn did.

Dale glared at Gwyn and spoke behind her back, "Come on Aslinn. It's time for us to go."

But Aslinn continued to move to the music, ignoring him. Dale grabbed her and spun her around. He took her by both arms and shook her, hoping to pull her out of her trance.

"Aslinn!" She wrapped her arms around him sleepily.

"Oh, Dale isn't it --"

Dale didn't give her time to finish. He pulled her through the dancers and headed toward the hall that Gwyllion had spoken of as the way out. He knew he couldn't trust her, but they couldn't stay here any longer either and he had to get Aslinn out of here quickly.

Just as they reached the entrance to the hall a fairy man who looked to be older than the rest, yet only

16

about thirty, stepped out from the wall. He wore dark blue satin fringed in shades of paler blue. His handsome face was unsmiling, but pleasant and he moved to stand in front of them.

Aslinn slumped in Dale's arms and he lifted her up against his side, revealing the ivy caught around his ankle and the fairy man glanced down at Dale's feet noticing it. Dale glared and took a step forward as he said, "Step aside."

With a calm and gentle voice though clearly warning he replied, "Do not go the way Gwyllion told you."

Dale kept Aslinn drawn near to him. She rested her groggy head against his shoulder. "And how do you know what she told me?"

"My name is Vitiris and I need only know that she would not tell you the truth."

Dale stared at him. *Mountain goddess, misleading travelers. Vitiris, god of wisdom.* It was coming back to him.

Vitiris gazed sadly upon Aslinn, "You may yet leave this place, but she cannot. She is already drunk with knowledge that cannot go into the Upper world."

"You lie!" *They are all fairies and not to be trusted*, he thought and Dale shoved past him and pulled Aslinn with him into the hall.

Vitiris called out to him. "It is good to be cautious, better to be wise. Look for the signs."

The stone castle walls of the long hall were bare, but for the occasional torch light in its sconce. There were doors that led to other rooms and many other halls that crossed this one. Dale began to feel despair at the thought of losing his way through the mass maze, but he kept going.

The cold dank dark seemed to consume the meager flames of the torches, making it darker, colder and Aslinn shivered in his arms. He felt chilled too so he pulled Aslinn close for her warmth.

They passed the first hall where Gwyllion had told him and then another and the farther they approached the end of the hall the darker it became. But just as they reached another branch of two halls that crossed this one Dale noticed something different.

The air here, although also cool, seemed lighter, fresher. Dale glanced down the hall to the left. It was brightly lit. He glanced down the hall to right, which was also well lit. He felt Aslinn stir.

"I want to go back to the dance. I'm hungry...and thirsty too. The wine was so sweet."

Dale's nerves prickled at the thought that she may have actually consumed some of the wine, but he hadn't seen her drink. Perhaps it was just the trance that made her think so. The smell of the food had seemed to carry taste into his mouth.

Aslinn tried to pull away from Dale, but he held her arm and pulled her back. He couldn't stop thinking of what she had said and his heart quickened. He hadn't seen Aslinn drink or eat anything, but what if she had. Is that why Vitiris had said she had knowledge that couldn't be taken into the upper world?

Dale peered down the dark hall straight ahead. Perhaps it wasn't too late if he could get them out quickly. He thought about Vitiris' warning, *"Look for the signs"*.

All the halls were well lit, but if he continued to go straight he would soon be in darkness. And so Dale decided to go on into the dark hall.

They moved from the light into the dark and soon it grew so dark that Dale could no longer see the way ahead of them. He let his shoulder brush against the wall to keep from stumbling in the darkness as he continued to drag Aslinn along with him, then suddenly he heard something. But what was it? It was a sound that seemed not to fit into this environment and so therefore, seemed unfamiliar. Dale moved further down the hall towards the sound. *Birds!*

Birds were chirping and Dale's heart quickened. He pulled Aslinn quickly through the darkness towards the sounds of chirping birds.

Aslinn stopped. Her voice told him she was still in a sleepy daze. "It's cold here, let's go back."

Fear and anguish gripped him without under-standing why. They were so close now, he knew it.

"No, Aslinn. We have to keep going. We have to get out of here."

Aslinn yanked away. It was more strength than he thought she had in her current state.

"I don't want to leave!"

Dale was stunned by her conviction. He yanked her hard and pulled her along. "You've been bewitched by the devil himself. I'm not leaving you here and I'm not staying."

The sounds of birds got louder and the thought of home so close filled Dale with tingling excitement.

Suddenly Dale noticed the air had changed. Although still cool it was damp and he realized they were in a mist. He rushed forward feeling light and numb with tingling excitement then he heard someone calling their names.

Dale moved through the mist until the mist grew bright. Moving from the darkness into sudden brightness made Dale's eyes sensitive. He put his hand up to his eyes until they were able to adjust to the bright light. When his eyes had adjusted and he lowered his hand, the town of Glastonbury stood clearly before him in the light of day. He was on the top of the Tor and the birds were chirping welcoming the sun which was bringing warmth into the early morning dawn. It was going to be a beautiful day.

Then Dale heard someone calling his name again in the distance. He heard it again and someone called "Aslinn..." and he turned to her.

Horror shook his limbs. He spun around. He was alone. His heart wrenched in anguish and he shouted, "Aslinn! Aslinn! Aslinn..." Dale fell on his hands and knees.

A strong gust of wind blew as if to exhale Dale's anguish twisting the ivy from around his ankle, which loosened then floated up, carried away in the breeze.

RECOMPENSE

In the narrow alley of a London apartment building the wind blows and scatters leaves up against the brick facade. One leaf soars in a spiraling gust and comes to rest upon the outer sill of a third floor window.

The early morning sun seeps through the dusty panes of the small bedroom. Starkly furnished, there is a plain wooden dresser with a framed mirror above it. To one side of the dresser resides a small framed photograph of a smiling woman with thick white hair pulled into a French twist bun. The sign above her head in the distance reads Paddington Station. On the other side is an open wooden cigar box that holds spending change, a wallet and car keys. Set squarely between them is a bible, its worn black cover and engraving faded with time and use.

Against the far wall, the covers are thrown back on a wrought iron bed with chipping green paint. Dale sits bent over on the edge of the bed and runs his hand through his hair in an effort to rub the sleep from his head.

He looks up. Youthful boyhood is long removed from his strong masculine face. He rubs at the dark stubble on his chin and glances to the one thing that adorns these otherwise blank walls -- a tattered framed poster of the Glastonbury Tor. White cracks run through its surface conveying momentary anguish but, the taped pieces now together again declare his need to prevail.

He ambles to the chair by the door. Draped neatly over the slatted wooden back is the uniform of a firefighter. The patch on his shirt shows his status as Station Officer.

Dale goes to the window and shoves on the sticky frame until it lets loose its onerous hold. Immediately the noises of the city coming to life greet him and the leaf floats to the floor in the cool breeze. He sticks his head out, inhales a deep breath of the cool morning air then heads for the bathroom to perform a quick shower and a shave before heading to work.

The cool tile beneath his bare feet quickly gives way to a soft towel at the shower stall in the small bathroom. Dale reaches in and turns the knob releasing a drizzle of water from the showerhead before relieving himself and returning.

He steps in and lets the water beat against his chest bringing him warmth then braces one arm against the shower wall and leans in to let the warm water run over his head and back awakening his tired muscles. He thinks about the day ahead and wonders what it will hold.

Dale hopes it won't be a quiet shift. He much preferred to be actively involved in the performance of the duties for which he had been trained. Of course, he didn't wish ill on anyone, but when things did happen he was ready and anxious to help. Truthfully, it was just too difficult for him to relax. He needed to be active in mind and body to brush the cobwebs away.

Dale slips the soap bar into its holder on the wall and turns to rinse the foam from his body before turning the knob to a slow drip. He makes two soggy footprints on the floor towel as he walks out and reaches for another towel to dry off then he wraps it around his waist and goes to stand in front of the sink. He reaches for his razor and stares up at his face in the mirror. So much time had passed, why did it still plague him as if it were yesterday?

Money had been tight after his father's death and Dale had always known that university would bring some hardship, but after Aslinn's disappearance and the towns ensuing accusations of his responsibility it became impossible for him to stay in Glastonbury. So, it wasn't long after those events that he reached the decision to become a firefighter.

Dale enjoyed training school and made good friends unaware of the events of his recent past. It helped, their not knowing and his not talking about it, to put it into his past, but like cobwebs no matter how often he swept them away they always came back.

Dale felt suited to his position and had moved swiftly up the ranks as Station Officer due not only to his natural skills in leadership and common sense, but to his many heroic efforts. Of course, Dale didn't consider himself a hero. No matter the personal peril or consequences of his actions, he always felt inadequate and undeserving of heroes praise for it was always too late. There would always be one he couldn't save.

Dale walks back into the bedroom in his socks and shorts, his lean muscular body still glistening with moisture. He dabs his chest and underarms then hangs the towel neatly on the empty arm of the chair.

Dale dresses in silence then goes to the dresser to retrieve his wallet and keys. He slips the change into his right front pocket and glances at the photograph of his mother then up at his reflection. Even without expression his eyes reveal a dark and mysterious scourge in his heart. His eyes avert to catch the reflection of the tattered poster. He bends his head and prays.

"Lord help me to prevail in all things set before me this day. In Christ's name I pray. Amen."

He sets his shoulders squarely, takes a deep breath and walks out the door. The sun shines deeply through the window pane in a white haze.

Mrs. Conklin leans back against her pillow and clutches a scrapbook in her lap. She turns her head to look out onto the view of the Tor in the distance. Agnes Dewar had opened the curtains when she brought up her breakfast tray, but she wishes she could shut out the sight of it now. Agnes was a good soul to spend so much of her time taking care of her now. Although she was some fifteen years younger, she had been a good friend to her, not blaming her for what happened to Dale, as she put it. Mrs. Conklin knew there would never be any convincing of anyone else and so it was a subject they both avoided.

She glances back out the window. The view had been one of the things she had loved about this house when they had first moved into it. Dale was only three then and so fascinated by it. That's when she had begun to tell him all the stories about the Tor. She recounted the tales of King Arthur and Lady Guinevere, when the Tor was called Avalon and of the destruction of the Church of St. Michael by the rare occurrence of earthquake leaving the only remaining remnant of the rebuilding after another earthquake, the tower. This of course, had led to the telling of the evil King of the Netherworld, Gwyn ap Nudd.

She told and retold, many times, the stories of the fairies, which Dale loved so much and she was sure it was God's will in this that had enabled him to escape all those years ago when Gwyn ap Nudd took his sweet Aslinn away and turned a bitter town against him. She could never again look upon the Tor without feeling the pain of loss, for the Perth's who lost their eldest daughter and for herself, but most of all for Dale.

Dale had had to leave, she understood that. If the townspeople had not believed him guilty of some wrongdoing in Aslinn's disappearance there would still be the Tor to remind him.

She didn't blame the townspeople for not believing in Dale's wild tale either. It was difficult enough at first for her to believe. But he was her son and a good boy. She had seen the torment in his eyes, felt it emerge from his heart. Dale had never wavered in his telling of what they had gone through, in what he described as no more than an hour at most, although the town had searched for them for three days before they found him. And she had always felt there was something special about Dale, as if he had some great purpose in life. Perhaps all mothers feel that way, but still she could not help but wonder if there was some connection to his purpose and the Tor.

Perhaps it was for the best that he had left, never to come back, she thought. It had certainly broadened her own experiences. Since her husband had died when Dale was ten it had been difficult to make ends meet. There hadn't been the kind of family holidays that most were known to enjoy.

Dale had never neglected her though. He called often and sent her money. He frequently made arrangements for them to meet and take holidays together and every time she went to visit him in London he would take her shopping, sightseeing or to the opera. Something they both enjoyed immensely.

Most of her memories of Dale were happy ones, but there was always that dark cloud that hung over him and that was what worried her now. She was dying, she knew, and she worried what would become of her beautiful son when there was no one left who believed in him.

Mrs. Conklin feels a clench in her chest, not with sickness of body, but of heart, and a stubborn tear she can't control rolls down her check. She reaches over to the bed stand and pulls a tissue from the box among the clutter of pill bottles. She dabs at her eyes quickly, not wanting Agnes or Doctor Hall to come in and find her crying.

Mrs. Conklin gazes back out at the Tor, then there is a knock. She looks toward the open door.

Doctor Hall carries his bag over and picks up the chair by the window and moves it beside her bed.

Although only in his thirties, Doctor David Hall is an old-fashioned physician. He had felt fortunate to acquire a small town practice, believing that every patient required a good dose of common sense and compassion as much as any medicine or treatment. Although he'd only been in Glastonbury for a few short years, he had become acquainted with and very fond of most of its residents.

He puts his bag on the chair and pulls the stethoscope from around his neck up.

"Don't know why you bother with that thing, I can tell you it's still beating and you should be able to tell when it's not. Besides, it's cold."

Doctor Hall smirks and lets it drop down on his chest.

"And good morning to you Mrs. Conklin."

He reaches for a thermometer in his pocket and holds it up to her.

"Do you mind? If I don't do something I'll feel like I wasted my parents' hard-earned money."

Mrs. Conklin chuckles, "They must be very proud of you."

He puts the thermometer in her mouth, nods humbly.

She smiles, rubs the scrapbook lovingly and he glances at it.

"What about your son?"

Her lip quivers, she clutches her hand around the scrapbook. Her automatic response is to look out at the Tor and he follows her gaze to the window.

Flames spew through the broken panes and charred frames caused by the combustible heat of the devastating inferno inside the run-down apartment building. The firefighters are busy at work clearing the building of its occupants and fighting the engulfing blaze.

Fire trucks line the street and onlookers stand at a distance to watch in excitement with a rare opportunity to be so close to such action. An elderly woman cries over the loss of all her worldly possessions. Others receive light medical attention and mill around dazed.

A news team strides through the crowd to capture pictures and interviews for their broadcast.

Dale, as the Station Officer, moves along the line of hoses, trucks and firefighters. When he sees Chris Stenroth exit the building removing his SCBA, self-contained breathing apparatus, as he approaches, he runs up to him. Chris is grimy with soot and followed by two other grimy firefighters. Dale knows they are Dan Jenks and Erin Vestle, but it's only Erin's six-four stature that enables him to tell them apart in their gear.

Chris comes up to Dale and shouts over the noises of diesel engines and spewing hoses. "The south end is contained, but the north wing is going fast."

Dale nods, and shouts back, "That's were it started, northwest corner. Witness says he saw smoke coming from a third floor flat..." Dale glances at the north end of the building and for a brief instant he sees the faint shadow of a figure through the smoke on the ground floor. Though the glimpse is brief and through the haze of smoke, the figure captures a familiar picture in his mind, Aslinn's long blonde hair; it was her face he saw. He dismisses the vision, but grabs his SCBA and points.

Chris looks to where Dale points and grabs his arm. "Too much falling debris...can't get through there."

But Dale rushes toward the building. Dan Jenks and Erin Vestle shake their heads then fall in behind Dale.

Dale rushes through the smoke haze of the first floor hall. The fire is moving down and spreading fast as large chunks of ceiling plaster and building frame crash down in burning rubble. So much is on the floor that it creates debris too difficult to crawl through and Dale nearly stumbles more than once as he crunches through it while he ducks the spewing flames and burning support beams that dangle overhead.

Although he can't see it, Dale hears the blast of water from the hose Dan and Erin have brought in behind him. Dirty water falls down on him as they direct their hose above him onto the burning embers.

Dale can't see anything moving through the smoke this way and feels his way along the wall. He reaches around one door frame then another and counts. *The next one should be it*, and he hopes he's calculated correctly.

Dale feels the door frame. He touches the door testing for heat of fire beyond it and tries the knob. It's locked. He pulls out his fire axe and begins to chop away at the door frame around the steel door. The frame splinters, gives way and Dale kicks the door open.

Fire is moving down through the ceiling here too and Dale kneels down and crawls toward the front of the building. He calls out, but there's no reply.

Dale's shoulder bumps against something and he hears the crash of glass as something falls to the floor. He maneuvers around other obstacles and follows the flow of smoke and flame toward the open window where he knows he will find his victim. The water soaked carpet squishes beneath his movements and Dale feels the rain of water come down on him from the blast of the hoses that shoots through the window toward the burning ceiling. It cuts a light mist through the haze that enables Dale to see and he crawls toward it. Then his knee brushes something solid. Dale reaches his hand out and crawls over to her. The sound of crumbling, crashing and smashing objects tells Dale he can't move back and he pulls her toward the window.

Chris waves to his men to move the hose away from the room they have been bombarding with water intermittently to hold back the flames in hopes that it will allow Dale to make his way through. He waits anxiously for a sign that Dale has reached it and is safe, then he sees it.

Dale waves his arm out the window and pulls the girl up. He leans her against him as he crawls through the window then hoists her over his shoulder. The sound of an ambulance siren undulates in the distance.

The thermometer beeps and Doctor Hall removes it from Mrs. Conklin's mouth and reads it.

"I'm proud of him too."

Doctor Hall looks up surprised. She hands him the scrapbook.

He puts the thermometer away. "You sure?"

She nods. "I know you've heard the stories. People got nothing better to do than to gab and gossip."

He takes the scrap book and opens it. There are photographs of Dale as a baby and as a small boy.

"Handsome lad." He turns the pages slowly.

She points to a bookmark. "That's where you'll find it."

He turns to the mark. There are newspaper clippings: Dale Conklin suspect in Aslinn Perth disappearance.

"No one believed him, of course. Difficult to, I know."

"Do you believe Mrs. Conklin?"

Her eyes hold the glint of mother's love. "He's my son...and a good man." She sniffs, dabs the tissue to her nose.

White smoke billows from the nearly extinguished burning building. Dale carries the limp form of a teenage girl. He lays her down, throws off his mask and begins CPR. The girl coughs. She begins to revive.

Dale closes his eyes in grateful relief. It gave him much needed restitution to save lives, but it would never be enough to remove his guilt for not being able to save Aslinn.

Paramedics come and lift the girl onto a gurney and he hears Chris' voice talking to him, but he doesn't know what he's saying. His mind is somewhere else as he watches them take the girl away, for every time he brought someone out of a burning building it was as if it was it were another opportunity to bring Aslinn out of hell. What would their lives had been like?

Doctor Hall couldn't help his special affection for this dear lady. She was strong in her emotions and sweet in her renderings. She never had an unkind thing to say about anyone, which reminded him of his Welsh grandmother. A woman he had only known as a child since she had died when he was twelve. But she was right about the gossip. He had heard the stories and others were not so kind.

He reaches his arm out, pats Mrs. Conklin's hand. "He should be here."

Mrs. Conklin's voice is strong with determination. "I'll not let him be humiliated and pounced upon by heathens."

Doctor Hall raises a surprised brow. "I thought you said you understood."

"I understand why they found it hard to believe. But I don't have to like how they treated him -- or me. Not a one of them had any sympathy for us."

"He's never returned here?"

She shakes her head, "It's been for the best, believe me. He sends me money and I visit him."

"But surely now..."

"When I'm in the ground he'll have no more reason to come back to Glastonbury."
She turns a stony face and Doctor Hall turns the page in the scrapbook. Another newspaper clipping: Aslinn Perth presumed dead, Conklin boy under psychiatric care.

Doctor Hall sits at his desk reading the clippings. It's a typical, if not small office, with medical books and magazines in a small bookcase. Prescription pads, notepads, a water bottle and a CD case with various prescription medicine names on them are on a credenza next to a computer.

Doctor Hall flips pages to the back of the scrapbook. Several more clippings indicate the heroic acts performed by Firefighter Dale Conklin and one small clipping indicates his promotion to Station Officer.

Surely this could not be a man capable of murder. It had been a long time since that horrible incident. He couldn't believe that there could be more than a few in this town who would begrudge a son his last opportunity to see his mother before she died. But he felt certain there may be at least one.

Doctor Hall sighs, rises and picks up his jacket. He glances down at the clippings in the scrapbook.

Articles are in layout for the latest edition of the Glastonbury Weekly Gazette. Beth Bryce looks over the spread for the latest weekly edition. It's loaded with small local events: a church bazaar, high school sports scores and Edna Symthe's winning recipe for plum preserves. Several books on Welsh folklore are held between book ends on her desk with a dictionary and thesaurus and there's a photograph of a girl about eight years old in a pewter frame at one corner of her desk beyond a stack of papers.

It's a small paper occupying a third of the space of the ground floor in the old downtown building. Three desks, two with computers, a small printing machine, copier, fax and file cabinets along the walls fill most of the space.

She's alone in the office and looks up as the bell over the door rings to see who it is. She's surprised at her discovery and calls out to him, "Afternoon, Doctor Hall."

"Beth, how's Lucy?"

Beth moves around the desk to greet him as he comes toward her. She's glad for a break and some company and gladder still that it's Doctor Hall. Lucy liked him, so she no longer had to drag her kicking and screaming when she required medical treatment. Beth likes him too. He's a good fit to their little community and has a much more pleasant demeanor than Doctor Hadley had had.

"Typical eight-year-old, in constant need of iodine and Band-Aids, but otherwise healthy and obstinate. Running low on patients?"

He laughs, "I trust my patients to come to me."

"So what brings you here?"

Doctor Hall glances around and notices that, thankfully, they are alone. He gazes down at the layout on her desk. It's difficult to get started not knowing what kind of reaction he might get, but he knows it needs to be done. Better there be no surprises. He looks up into Beth's curious face.

"I came to speak with you about Mrs. Conklin."

Beth's interest goes from casual to intense. She'd heard Mrs. Conklin had been ill.

"She's dying, Beth."

Beth's heart pounds, she feels weak with anticipation. "Has this got something to do with Aslinn's death? Has she said something?"

Doctor Hall points her to a chair. Beth goes for it hungrily not knowing if her knees will hold. Her hands begin to shake at the thought that Mrs. Conklin may have possibly revealed some secret truth on wishing to clear a guilty conscience. After all these years, would she finally know what had become of her sister, Aslinn?

Doctor Hall sits beside her. He notices the tremor in Beth's movement, the wild-eyed curiosity. His worst suspicions have been confirmed and he wonders what kind of reaction others in town might have when they learn the news.

"Your sister's disappearance and the story Dale Conklin told about it are almost a legend here, but you were so young when it happened. I didn't expect it would still affect you so strongly."

"I adored him almost as much as Aslinn did, then to..." She bites her lip. She wants to scream, *Tell me! Tell me what she's told you,* and she begins to think of how she would go about making arrangements to lay Aslinn's bones to rest.

Doctor Hall takes a breath. This is going to be much more difficult than he had anticipated.

"She's his mother, Beth. I thought it only right that he have a chance to say good-bye."

Her expression freezes in wide-eyed shock. Her breath stills, then she softly mutters, "Dale Conklin is coming to Glastonbury?"

Beth rises. She feels a need to...do something, but she really hopes that something isn't to faint. She goes to the window and stares out. Her throat has suddenly gone dry and she doesn't want to try to speak. Could she bear to see him again? Time heals wounds, but these were cut deeply and left protruding scars. Beth feels her wounds rip open again at the thought of Dale returning to Glastonbury.

Doctor Hall moves toward her, but Beth turns a stony face at him.

"This is not good news Doctor, but it will most certainly make news if he comes here. There are still too many people who remember what he did."

"What he's believed to have done. There was never any proof."

"You weren't here."

"Do you know he's had an exemplary career as a firefighter? Some would even consider him a hero."

Beth's incensed. "A hero? That's not what they call him here, Doctor Hall. Murderer! There is no other word for it."

"I'm sorry for your pain, Beth, truly I am. But I still think it was the right thing to do. I just thought you should know."

She turns away again, stares out the window. "I didn't get a chance to say goodbye to my sister."

Doctor Hall gazes at her. He had really believed, or maybe just hoped that it would be different. Beth had suffered the loss of her sister, the death of her parents in an automobile accident and then a husband that had abandoned her and wouldn't offer any help in the raising of their child. It didn't seem fair to inflict any more pain upon her. But then it didn't seem fair that Mrs. Conklin should have to die without her last goodbye to her only son either.

Sometimes, he thought, *to cure a pain in one heart you have to inject a little into another.* Now his hopes are that Beth's pain will dissolve again quickly. There is nothing else to say although he wishes he could think of something. *Best to leave her to her thoughts,* and he turns to walk away.

Beth's thoughts take her back in time. She hears the bell over the door ring and Doctor Hall's steps get fainter and the rhythm of a ticking clock fills her mind.

The striped wing backed chair swallowed Beth's small frame. Her feet dangled over, unable to reach to floor. Adults hovered in small groups and spoke in low whispers and the clock on the mantel beside her ticked loudly in the hushed quietness of the crowded room.

She watched her mother and tried desperately to understand how she should feel, how she should act, but it was too confusing.

Friends greeted her mother, hugged her and she smiled at them and thanked them for coming, then suddenly she would break into tears and sob. Beth had wished Dale were there with her, but she knew everyone was angry at him, especially her father and she couldn't understand why. Beth wanted Aslinn to come back and she wanted things to get back to normal again. Since Aslinn had gone her mother was always sad and her father constantly angry, snapping at her for reasons she couldn't understand and making her a prisoner in her own home. School had become her only refuge from the oppressive nimbus that hung over them there.

Beth knew about the accusations that Dale had killed Aslinn, but she knew that it wasn't true. She knew it because she knew Dale. She loved him. Aslinn teased her about it calling it a crush, but Beth did love Dale. Maybe it wasn't in the same way, as Aslinn had said, but it was love and she was just as hurt by the bawdy conjecture as to what had happened to Aslinn as she was by their belief that Dale had had anything to do with it. How could anyone believe that Dale would do something so horrible?

But time had gone on. Aslinn had not returned and conjecture grew doubt, confusion and eventually hate for her parents and the townspeople. They had never been able to prove anything, but they would never forget or forgive Dale. Even long after Dale had left Glastonbury Aslinn's disappearance continued to be the favored gossip around town. Eventually even Beth could no longer remember a reason not to believe as everyone else did. He had betrayed her love and trust and she had grown to hate him as much or more than anyone else could.

A car shifts into first gear at the stop sign at the corner. The clutch grinds and brings Beth back to the present. She glances at the clock. Lucy would be getting out of school soon. Then Beth turns to look back out the window and watches the car that motors through the street outside.

There is light traffic on road to Glastonbury in the late afternoon. The long drive had been like a journey into the past as Dale's thoughts had been consumed with his memories of living and growing up there. *You can't go home again. Who said that,* he thought, but then he decided it didn't really matter, the intention was certainly not the same.

Dale's thoughts went to the people he knew and had been fond of and of Aslinn, of course. But for as much as he tried to brace himself for whatever lay ahead he was not prepared for his first glimpse of the Tor.

Dale's heart constricts at the sight of it looming before him in the distance. His eyes are drawn to it and a car horn blares signaling he has drifted into the other lane. Dale swerves the car back into its proper lane and his eyes find the Tor again. He pulls over to the side of the road and stops.

His hands clench the steering wheel making his knuckles white. He closes his eyes and in a low whisper he speaks to her. "Aslinn...I'm so sorry, so..." A tear slides down his cheek. He wipes it away angrily. He can't let this place and its past draw him back into the torments of hell he has worked so hard and so long to expel himself from.

Dale thinks of the phone message that was waiting for him when he arrived back at the station after this morning's fire. He was sure the news was bad when he saw that is was a doctor in Glastonbury that had called. He's grateful that the doctor called him and he knows why his mother wouldn't and guilt consumes him.

It must have been hard on her to continue to live in Glastonbury with the speculation and accusations she had to endure on his behalf. *What will people do when they find out I'm in town. Maybe they'll leave us alone, under the circumstances, knowing I'll never have any reason to come back again.* But he doesn't really believe that.

He knows that it's far more likely they will torment her remaining days by their spiteful actions regardless of how much he tries to avoid or ignore them. But there's no decision to be made. Whatever the cost, how could he do anything else but be with his mother when he owes her so much. She was always the only one who believed in him.

Dale puts the car in gear and pulls back onto the road as the sun sets on the Tor.

Mrs. Conklin lies propped up in bed and gazes at the Tor through the window. Agnes removes the dinner tray from her lap and smiles with a glint in her eye.

"You have a visitor."

Her eyes feel as heavy as her heart. "I don't feel up to it."

Agnes nods toward the door. "Oh, I think you'll feel up to this one." Mrs. Conklin turns her gaze to the door. Her heart leaps.

Dale stands at the door and smiles at her, though his heart is heavy to see her that way. She looks so weak and weary. He waits for Mrs. Dewar to pass and she doesn't hide her distain for him when she glowers at him as she does. Dale closes the door behind her. He's not concerned with how Mrs. Dewar feels about him or anyone else.

He goes over to his mother and she reaches her arms up to hug him with tears of joy in her eyes. Dale puts his arms around her and it occurs to him how fragile she feels. He sits down on the bed beside her and takes her hand.

"You shouldn't be here."

"What's this? I thought you'd be glad to see me."

She rests back against her pillow tiredly and wipes the tears on her face. He reaches for a tissue on the night table and hands it to her. She can't take her eyes off him and puts her hand on his.

"You know I am, but --"

"Nothing could keep me away, Mother, no one in this town, the Tor nor even Gwyn ap Nudd himself."

She gapes in horror. He smiles, pats her hand.

"Don't you worry about me."

"How can I not, you're my child."

"I'm a grown man."

"Makes no difference."

Her eyes narrow in an obstinate gaze. "That bothersome doctor's the one that's done this."

Dale smiles, it's reassuring to know she hasn't lost her spirit. "And I'm grateful to him. You should have told me you were ill."

She wishes the doctor had minded his own business as much as she'd like to kiss him for bringing Dale here, but now that he is her heart breaks with the thought of how Dale will be treated and she wishes she

40

could protect him from that. "That bothersome doctor", she mutters.

It's been an emotional journey and an emotional reunion with his mother and Dale can't fight the tears that begin to well up in his eyes so he lowers them hoping she won't see, but she does. She touches his face with her soft hand.

"I'm so sorry for the trouble I've brought you."

She strokes his hair. "You never brought me anything but joy."

Dale smiles at her lovingly. He knows that it's far from true and it torments him. She deserved so much better than he had been able to provide.

He chokes back his pain, pats her hand and rises. "Get some rest."

"But you just got here."

"And I'm not going anywhere. You're tired, I heard you say so yourself. I'll be back to check on you in a little while." He bends down, kisses her cheek, whispers, "I love you."

She watches him go to the door knowing that it's been difficult for him to return to Glastonbury...so many memories. He turns and glances back at her before closing the door, but she continues to stare at it still feeling his presence, knowing he is here...home, then that feeling of connection pierces her heart and she turns an apprehensive glance back to the dark silhouette of the Tor.

Beth sits at the dining room table and gazes out the window. Her reflection shines back at her mirrored by the still darkness beyond and the bright overhanging light, but it's the reflection of her life she sees in her mind.

So much time has passed, so many things have happened. Raising a small child alone is a difficult thing even in a small town, and she wonders will she see him while he's here? What if she should, what would she do? So many unanswered questions, would she have the strength to ask them now? Could she utter any sound not suffused with hatred.

The sound of Lucy's footsteps in the hall bring her out of her daze and she quickly busies herself, clearing two dinner plates from the table. She can't let Lucy know that she's disturbed; she has to protect her from all of this if she can.

Lucy comes up beside her, a furry undressed Paddington Bear in her arm. Her hair is pulled back into two ponytails making her bright inquisitive eyes look larger.

"I can't find Paddy's sleep shirt."

Beth strokes Lucy's face. She was just about that age when she lost her sister. Now, Lucy is all she has left in this world.

"I suppose he has to have it if he's going to an overnight slumber with you."

Lucy nods and Beth puts the plates down. She gives Lucy a stern glance. "What did I say about keeping his things together?"

Lucy glances up sheepishly. "I'm striving for perfection, Mum, but I'm only eight -- it's sure to take more time."

Beth smothers laughter and hugs Lucy to her then takes her face in her hand. "You're closer than you think, Lucy girl." Lucy grins.

"Come on, then, let's find Paddy's sleep shirt. We can't have him going round improperly dressed. They move out of the kitchen and down the hallway toward Lucy's room.

42

Pictures and photographs line the hallway walls and Beth pauses to look at a photograph of her and Aslinn taken on the top of the Tor only months before her disappearance.

She glances back to see Lucy go into her room and plop down on her bed, her tiny legs dangling over the edge. Beth's heart aches with the thought of losing Lucy. Though she is yet still a child, she knows that someday the time will come when she'll have to let her go. Whatever will she do then? She sighs at the thought and walks through the door into Lucy's bedroom.

With yellow wallpaper dotted with the characters from The Hundred Acre Forest, Beth wonders if it was a natural progression that led her from Winnie the Pooh to Paddington. All the stuffed Pooh characters were about with Lucy's other toys, but it was Paddington she couldn't do without.

Lucy hums a little tune and puts Paddington into a little dance on her lap. "Do you think it will rain tomorrow?"

Beth notices Paddington's suitcase open on the bed next to Lucy's, his rain suit and boots lie on top.

"It's always good to be prepared."

Beth goes to the dresser, opens a drawer and rummages through it. "Ah hah." Beth pulls out the sleep shirt and holds it up.

"How'd you find it so quickly?"

Beth takes the shirt over to Lucy and hands it to her. "The difference in looking and not, I think." Beth looks through Lucy's overnight bag.

"Got everything?" Lucy nods.

"How about a big hug and kiss for your mum?

Lucy complies generously and Beth holds on tight. Old fears mix with new ones. *Why do things have to change? Why couldn't they just stay the way they are right now? How could Dale have betrayed her and Aslinn...What turned him into such an evil monster? Would she recognize him if she saw him?*

Beth realizes her hug has been a long one as Lucy squirms in her arms so she brings her arms down to look at her. "All mine?"

"All yours, Mum."

Beth continues to hold Lucy at arm's length. She wants to hug her tight again, needs the comfort of Lucy near her, but she's afraid to let her know she's troubled. What will Dale's presence do to this town? Will she be strong enough to survive an upheaval of the past in the present? How will she explain it all to Lucy if she asks?

The faint sound of a hounds howl in the distance breaks into Beth's thoughts and sends a shiver through her.

Dale sits on the porch stairs. The night is still. He glances around to the quaint homes along the street and imagines the unencumbered existence beyond the walls of lighted rooms -- families together chatting, watching television, praying together before a meal. He used to know these people...in these houses. There was warmth in their homes and their hearts then.

His gaze goes to the small green house across the street. It used to be yellow and he remembers that Mr. Castleberry used to keep a milking goat, Henry. Dale never cared for the milk, but he liked the cheese sandwiches Mrs. Castleberry prepared for him and Charles when they played together at their house on Saturday afternoons.

Dale chuckles as he glances down the street and remembers the time when Henry had got loose and ate through nearly every flower bed and vegetable garden on the street. Mrs. Husketh nearly fainted when she saw the result in her prize rose garden. From that time forward the goat had been referred to as Henry the eighth for his frolicking beheading of every living plant in his path.

Dale's gaze drifts upward. There are only a few thin clouds to filter the star-filled sky and he prays for peace in this town and for strength to endure loneliness unlike he has ever endured before. For even though they had been separated by time and distance, he had always known his mother was there. Soon, however, he knew that would no longer be true.

His gaze drifts down and he stares at the Tor through the darkness. Then suddenly, from its very peak it seems, Dale hears the mournful howl of a hound. His hand clinches tight against an uncontrollable shudder and he whispers, "No...no."

RECRIMINATION

Doctor Hall sits on the stool in his examination room and writes out a prescription. His patient, Sam Flye wheezes with every breath as he buttons his shirt. Doctor Hall tears the prescription off the pad and spins the stool around just in time to watch Sam tuck in his tails. He looks at the cigar in Sam's shirt pocket as he hands over the little slip of paper.

"It will help if you lay off the cigars."

Sam opens his mouth to expound his rebuttal and a choir of voices rings out from the street outside. The two men stare at each other in startled irony then glance toward the window. They are upon it within seconds and Doctor Hall yanks the blind cord, drawing it up to expose a full view to the street.

Cars and people pack the street with more forming with every business they pass. Car horns blare at the pedestrians that block their way. Sam's wheezes make it difficult to understand what is being said and they watch as the crowd draws nearer until they move in clear sight past the clinic and their words become clear.

"Murderer! Hang him! Monster! Conklin's a kiddie killer!" Doctor Hall's face goes white.

"Looks like a blooming lynch mob." Sam grabs his jacket off the hook behind the door and rushes out.

Doctor Hall continues to stare out at the crowd. He can't believe these simple folk in this quaint town could hold such a terrible grudge. It's been more than twenty years and yet they behave as if it were something that had happened only yesterday.

He pulls off his lab jacket and tosses it on the stool, but he doesn't notice or doesn't care that it slips to a crumpled heap on the floor. Doctor Hall's long strides take him out of the examine room and down the short hall into the waiting room in seconds. How could he have misjudged the people of this town so?

Shirley, his receptionist and his nurse Sharon are pinned to the window in the waiting room with another woman, probably his next patient. They ignore the incessant ringing phone and Doctor Hall is too anxious to leave to stop and scold them. His brief perusal determines that if she is his next patient she looks well enough to wait. At the moment it is this madness in the street that is a dire emergency, for there's no backing out of his responsibility in this horrible nightmare and he must go and do whatever he can to help set it right.

He calls out as he rushes past the women, "Cancel my morning appointments and page me if you need me."

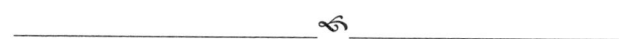

Agnes Dewar prepares a breakfast tray in the small crowded kitchen. There would be no more than three steps to anything in every direction, but for the round Formica topped table in the center, which made one have to go in circles around it.

She lifts the tea kettle off the stove and shuffles a half-step to the counter between it and the sink. Unsure if she heard something, she glances out the window over the sink, but not hearing anything else she pours water from the tea kettle into the small tea pot. She stiffens when she hears Dale walk in, glances up briefly then quickly busies herself with the tray.

Dale had sensed Mrs. Dewar's disdain for him, but being in such close quarters he certainly couldn't avoid her. He would try his best to stay out of her way when she was in, he decided, but he wasn't going to act like a criminal.

"Mrs. Dewar, I didn't hear you come in."

Her voice is cold and she doesn't look at him, but just reaches for the sugar dish as she says, "I try not to be a bother."

Dale knows the attitude, but it's something he hasn't had to face for some time. He supposes it will be this way with everyone he sees while in Glastonbury, but he won't return their disdain.

It was something his mother had taught him back then, "*Just ignore them. Keep your head up and walk past*" and there had only been a few times when Dale was forced to defend himself physically. Now, he hopes, tempers have been subdued by time and any new troubles can be avoided.

"I appreciate all you've done for my mother."

She picks up the tray, turns and really looks at him for the first time. He was always such a handsome, charming boy. It never made any sense how he got to be...

She starts around the table and snips, "No reason I shouldn't just because --"

Dale stares, waits for her to finish her sentence. He won't back down either, but she purses her lips tight and looks down at the tray in her hands.

"Well, just the Christian thing to do, is all."

The voices of the crowd draw their attention. Dale squeezes past her to the door and looks out. Agnes sets the tray down on the table and moves to the window over the sink and peers out. The crowd moves toward them and their shouts become clearer.

Agnes mumbles, "Knew this would be a mistake."

Dale glances over at Mrs. Dewar. She snubs her nose at him, turns and picks up the tray and walks out. Dale turns his attention back to the crowd. *"A mistake."* How many times had his mind played over the events that led up to Gwyn ap Nudd transporting he and Aslinn into Annwn? *If they hadn't gone to the Tor that day...if they hadn't taunted Gwyn with claims of being king and queen of his domain...if Dale had not derided Gwyn in disbelief...if he had believed...*

What was their mistake? Was there ever anything that could have prevented it from happening? He stares out at the crowd moving toward his mother's house. This is something he certainly never expected and he glances upward to where he knows his mother lies in bed hearing the same defaming calls and anger fills him. Dale opens the door and walks outside.

Dale watches the mob approach with stern determination from the small porch steps that lead down to a narrow walkway and out into the street. Someone in the crowd sees him, points and yells, "There he is!"

The throng rushes forward and another voice screams, "Get him," but when Dale steps forward the crowd stops.

"Let my mother die in peace and I promise never to return."

An angry looking man in a hunting cap and jacket with a baseball bat moves forward. "Did Aslinn Perth die in peace?" A few men start forward again behind the man in the hunting cap and Dale notices that several of them have weapons of some sort, boards, chains...rope? What were they planning a lynching? But the wailing siren of an approaching police car seems to give them second thought and they stop short.

Dale closes his eyes in brief relief then scans through the crowd. He recognizes only a few, but he's sure there are many more there that he used to know. People change through the years and it had been a long time. That thought made him clench his teeth. That they could carry such a grudge for something that he had never done and they could only presume.

The police car inches through the crowd separating them and pulls up in front of the house. Dale is relieved to have some assistance by the two constables that get out, but they ignore the verbal abuses and angry mob and walk straight up the path toward Dale.

Doctor Hall pushes through the crowd. He'd had to park his car down the street not able to move quickly enough through the throng and as he reaches the walk to Dale's house he's nearly knocked down by John Battersby who pushes past.

Battersby's face is flushed, his eyes bulge in hatred as he rushes past the two constables and jumps onto the porch with flailing fists. Dale captures the angry blows before they make their bruising impact and struggles to hold him off without bringing his own blows against Battersby, even though it's his first instinct in his own enraged state.

Dale can tell the man is blind with rage, it will be better if the police handle this. No need to give these people more to complain about.

Battersby senses the constables behind him and stops his flailing long enough to spit out his words. "Where is she? Tell me what you've done with her?"

Dale gapes. He's not sure he even knows this man and can't think why he should be so incensed. Then Battersby reaches for a choke hold on Dale and Dale is forced to twist the man's arms behind his back. He tries to hold him, but Battersby is a big man and his continuous struggle to free himself nearly knocks Dale off his feet. Dale releases him with a shove that sends him tottering at the brink of the stairs.

"Leave me alone -- all of you!"

Battersby catches his balance, his senses are still out of control when he rushes up on Dale again. This time the officers grab his arms and pull Battersby off another attack on Dale.

Dale let's his feelings loose, "It's about time."

Constable Griffith's tone is soothing when he speaks to Battersby, "You're upset Mr. Battersby, let us handle this."

He's upset, Dale thinks. *What about my mother, what about me? Is this whole town mad?* Battersby relaxes his shoulders and Griffith releases him. Without a moment's hesitation Battersby jumps at Dale again. This time he manages to throw Dale against the wall in a thud.

Battersby's face is so close that Dale can feel his breath when he whispers, "I'll kill you if you've hurt her."

Both constables rush up to pull Battersby away. This time Griffith keeps his restraint on Battersby and leads him away while Constable Churchwell stays with Dale.

Dale's dazed from the physical onslaught. That must also explain his confusion. *Did he say, "If you've hurt her?"* Dale sweeps his hand out at the crowd, "My mother's very ill constable."

"Under the circumstances I think it might be best if you come along with us, Mr. Conklin."

Doctor Hall climbs the porch steps and moves cautiously past Battersby and Constable Griffith. Constable Churchwell turns a wary glance at Doctor Hall as he approaches, but just as he's about to say something Doctor Hall gives voice to Dale's thoughts. "What's the reason for this?"

Constable Churchwell gives him an irritated glare. "Who are you?"

Doctor Hall glances at Dale. They had never met and only briefly spoken on the phone and now he was unsure of how welcome he may be, having brought all this misery upon Mrs. Conklin and Dale, not to mention the entire town of Glastonbury. They may all ride him out on a rail.

"I'm Doctor David Hall...and a friend of the family."

"Well it's just a formality at this time you understand, but given the situation --"

There's that phrase again! Dale grits his teeth, incensed. "What situation? I haven't been in this town for twenty-five years, I'm back one night and --"

"Which is just precisely what makes this whole thing so...interesting...since you brought it up."

Now Doctor Hall's patience is worn through. "Make sense man -- what are you talking about?"

"The missing children."

The words fall like a stone. Dale's breath seizes in his chest, the blood rushes from his head. The doctor gapes, horrified. *The missing children.* Battersby loses control again and struggles in Constable Griffith's grasp.

"I'll kill you Conklin! I'll do worse to you than you've done to them. I promise you that. Do you hear?"

The crowd becomes fueled again by Battersby's outburst. They begin to scream and shout. Dale's eyes roll to heaven. He thinks back to last night when he heard the hound on the Tor.

"Please dear God, don't let this happen again. Help me find an end to this."

Doctor Hall watches Dale. How could he have been so wrong? Was he wrong? Well it was now evident that one of the children was Evelyn Battersby, but who was the other child? A hollow pit in his stomach lurched as he voiced the question, "Who are the children?"

The constable stares straight into Dale's eyes as he delivers the answer, "Evelyn Battersby and Lucy Bryce."

Doctor Hall's heart fills the pit in his stomach as the blood rushes from his face. "No..." It was barely audible and the sound of his own voice is unfamiliar in his ears. He gazes at Dale. Is that the face of a monster? Is he responsible for this by bringing Dale Conklin here? The din of the crowd is a low echo in his ears against his own guilty thoughts. He had always been such a good judge of people's character.

Doctor Hall looks for the truth of his rash judgment in Dale's face, but when he does it seems that the look on Dale's face mimics the way he himself feels. No, he decides, as he looks back into the angry faces of the crowd. *I will not make my judgment on him without evidence. I must learn the truth and accept responsibility for any part I've had in it.*

Doctor Hall shifts in the hard wooden chair. He looks around the small local police station. All the chairs seem to offer the same level of discomfort and he tries to find a comfortable position against the ache in his back, shoulders and numb bum. Tension...a muscle relaxer and a hot bath would be his prescription for someone else. He chuckles to himself as he suddenly realizes for a man who seldom drinks it's precisely one stiff one he would demand for himself right now in lieu of the opportunity for the other. He glances at his watch, eleven o'clock. Bit early for that yet, good thing, perhaps the urge will pass on principle.

He had checked on Mrs. Conklin before leaving Dale's house and coming here. She was, of course, terribly distraught and although she had plenty of reason to blame him she hadn't said a word. Somehow that only served to add to his guilt, but he had felt his previous convictions of Dale's innocence while with her and he had promised to do what he could to help before giving her a sedative and leaving her to sleep.

He gazes at the interior office door with the large pane of textured glass on top. Painted letters label the room "Interrogation" and for as much as he tried he still couldn't make out the vague figures that move beyond the distorted glass.

He had been told that an inspector from London had come to question Dale and he was sure they had been in that room for some time already well before he got here. Doctor Hall pulls his pager from its clip at his belt and checks for messages. He had canceled all his appointments for today, but as the only doctor in town he has responsibilities to his patients and his concerns for Mrs. Conklin are now greater than ever.

He shakes his head in disdain for what she's being put through in her final hours. There should have been joy and peace, not this.

A door opens at the end of the hall. He's grown accustomed to the ramblings of all the people in the station since he's been here for what...two hours? Soon, he knew, the place would be full of reporters. The phones had been ringing off the hook from newspapers and television stations from as far as London all morning.

Doctor Hall continues his vigilant stare at the textured glass window on the door and at first he doesn't notice except that a figure passes in front of him. Then he sees that it's Beth and jumps to his feet. He sprints up behind her.

"Beth! I'm so sorry --"

Beth turns a stone face at him and in less than a blink he feels the sting of her hand against his face. It freezes him in mid motion and he stares at her taught jaw and watches as tears begin to well up in her already red, swollen eyes before she swiftly turns and walks away. Then as if some hand of fate were willing it, the door to the interrogation room opens right in front of her and Dale walks out.

Now Beth knew the answer to one question, the answer is right in front of her. His features are more defined, but distinctive as ever, the large brown eyes, dark heavy brows, straight nose thick lips and square jaw. Beth's feet stick to the dingy linoleum as if they

56

are stuck in concrete. She stares and watches Dale move toward Doctor Hall. Of course he wouldn't recognize her, she was so young, but there was no mistaking him.

It had been so hard for Dale to concentrate on the details of the questioning; his mind was riddled with concern for how all this was affecting his mother. Would her weak heart give in to the break and pain she must be feeling now.

The first familiar face he sees is that of Doctor Hall and the shock on his face tells him his concerns were more than valid, but he has to ask the question.

Dale's movements feel to slow to be real, but the flail of tiny beating fists on his back spins him around in quick time and he catches Beth's wrists in his hands.

His heart pounds with a fierce ache as he holds her there and stares into Beth's face. She groans through clenched teeth, her face streaked with tears. He knows who this woman is. She's the mother of the other missing child, Beth Bryce. No one has to tell him, he can see it in her eyes and his heart fills with compassion. If only he could take away her pain and his, and bring back the children.

She stares at him with what seems like understanding for just an instant. It gives Dale hope that he was able to communicate his sorrow, but quickly the hatred fills her eyes again and she yanks her wrists from his clasp.

"What have you done with my baby? Why are you doing this to me? Aslinn -- now my Lucy. Why?!"

Beth pounds a fist into his chest and he accepts it, hoping it will give her some release of her agony. She stops and he takes her fists in his hands and pulls them down.

Beth shakes with pain and anger. She keeps her gaze on the floor not wanting to look into his face...Dale's face and someone she once loved so long ago. But all those feelings were long gone. She hated him now, she had to hate him.

A voice inside her head screams at her, *Look at what he is not at what you, in a little girl's fantasy, had once believed him to be.* She lifts her gaze back to his face. This time she will see the monster.

Dale's heart breaks for her as he looks into her tear swollen eyes and he suddenly realizes a faint resemblance. Dale shakes his head against the possibility. "Beth?" Not the little girl he used to ride on the handlebars of his bicycle...the princess of the Tor.

The Inspector, like everyone else had been watching intently, waiting for some clue, slip of words or reaction. Doctor Hall had been afraid to try, but it's now clear no one else is going to step in. They're too intent on waiting for something to happen, too curious to see the scene play out. He reaches for Beth's arm and Dale releases her to him.

Dale steps back and watches his nightmare grow deeper into the pit of hell.

Beth still holds her gaze on Dale and Doctor Hall tries to pull her from her trance. She's over wrought, exhausted and in shock. "Beth, please..." Doctor Hall feels her tremble and he catches her as her legs begin to give way and he leads her to a chair. She begins to cry uncontrollably.

Dale's words seem more for himself than anyone else, but she hears them just the same. "God grant us both the strength to survive this nightmare again."

Beth looks over at Dale through her haze of tears. He stares compassionately. She pleads. "Please bring her back to me," before collapsing in Doctor Hall's arms in uncontrollable sobs.

There's nothing Dale can say. He looks around the room. The phones have been ringing and yet no one had wanted to divert their attention from the drama that had played out before them. Now it appears they want to avoid him as they slowly move back to their individual desks or tasks. Only Inspector Rudolph is left glaring with a steely gaze and crossed arms, but Dale doesn't say another word, he just turns and walks down the hall toward the back exit.

Beth's sobs have quieted to a snivel and she blows her nose with Doctor Hall's ever ready handkerchief. He glances up at the inspector inquisitively.

"He's free to go?"

The inspector's eyes never leave Dale's back. "For now."

Beth peers at the inspector wanting an explanation, but knowing there is none that will satisfy her, Doctor Hall or anyone else, it's all too much so she jumps up and runs for the front door.

Doctor Hall exhales an exhausted sigh and sprints for the back exit behind Dale. He's no longer sure of what he should do, just that he must do something.

Dale and Doctor Hall walk up to the house. Graffiti covers the façade in bold letters: MURDERER, KIDDIE KILLER.

Dale stops and stares at the words and Doctor Hall watches him for his reaction, but there is none and he's not sure what that means.

"You all right?"

Dale glances at the upstairs window. "How's my mother?"

Doctor Hall follows his gaze to the window. "Surprisingly strong when I left her."

Dale looks for some answer in the doctor's face. He smiles and pats Dale's shoulder. "Determination to help you, I expect. Medicine cannot define what the heart and mind can render."

Dale sits exhaustedly on the stairs and stares out blankly. A car, occupied by teenage boys approaches and motors by slowly. They throw out obscenities and a bottle, which smashes near Dale's feet as they pass.

Glasses clang together on the bar of the West End Pub as the bartender sets three ales down. Brian picks up the ales and takes them to a table where Battersby and another man, Ridley, sit finishing their ales. He sets the drinks down and joins them. Battersby, in a daze, looks out, but at no one as he speaks.

"How they could just let him go is beyond me. He's only here one day and does this...what more will he do?"

Ridley takes up the full glass and snidely remarks, "They never found no evidence before. There's no evidence a crime's been committed they say."

The men watch Battersby silently. They know his violent temper will surface and strike again. Ridley's ready for it. He loves a good fight and so he urges him. "We know he's done it."

Brian gulps a long swig, "The whole town knows he's the one's done it."

Battersby stares off, mumbles "No evidence." He takes a long draw and downs the ale.

Brian gulps his ale in an effort to keep up. "You think he'll get away with it again?"

Battersby's eyes shoot over at him then he peers at Ridley with a wicked smile. "Not this time."

Ridley's mouth curves up and Brian surveys them curiously. They're cooking something up for sure and he's dying to find out what.

There is a closed sign on the door of the Glastonbury Weekly Gazette. Beth sits at her desk and stares out, Lucy's Paddington is clutched tight in her arms still dressed in his sleep shirt. "Please God...please bring Lucy back to me."

Beth stares down at the archived articles surrounding Aslinn's disappearance and tears well up in her eyes.

Doctor Hall takes Mrs. Conklin's blood pressure while Dale sits at her other side and holds her hand. Doctor Hall shakes his head as he removes the apparatus from her arm. It sends Dale into alarm.

"What's wrong?"

Doctor Hall pauses as he puts it away in his bag and looks at Mrs. Conklin.

"I wish I could take credit for your improved good health." He glances at Dale. "But I have a feeling it has more to do with your influence."

Dale shakes his head. "I don't see how. I've brought you all this trouble again."

She smiles at him. "Shush, now. You weren't responsible then and you're not responsible now. It's these heathens and their narrow-minded notions...they're the ones."

Dale shakes his head, smiles lovingly at her, pats her hand. Doctor Hall gathers his bag and heads for the door.

"Get some rest now. If you keep improving this way, I'll be taking you for fish and chips at Knights by weekend."

Mrs. Conklin winks at Dale. "Be careful what you ask for, Doctor. I haven't had a date in so long I'm likely to hang around just for the opportunity."

Doctor Hall and Dale chuckle then Dale kisses her cheek and rises.

"Be good and do what he says."

Dale goes to the door and pulls it to, then follows Doctor Hall down the stairs and into the kitchen.

Doctor Hall lays his medical bag on the table. He's not really anxious to go, but doesn't know how to approach Dale. He wants desperately to talk to him and try to glean some understanding of events present and past. He watches Dale reach for the tea kettle on the stove then go to the sink to fill it with water and looks for a way to begin.

"How about some tea, Doctor Hall?"

He's glad the opportunity availed itself, "I wouldn't mind."

Dale feels somewhat relaxed for the first time since the whole business started. He glances at the clock. *Was it just this morning? It feels like eternity.*

Doctor Hall sits exhaustedly and watches Dale prepare things for the tea. It occurs to him that Dale has the appearance of someone of a calm, quiet nature. But then it occurs to him that serial killers are often thought of that way.

Dale sits down at the table and stares at the salt and pepper shakers. He reaches for the salt and fiddles with it. He feels a bond of friendship with Doctor Hall could be possible if only these circumstances hadn't gotten in the way. In only the brief time since they'd met he'd been very kind to him, he'd not prejudged him and not even asked any questions. He had just been there.

Dale fiddles with the shaker while Doctor Hall glances about. They are both trying to find words to say and finally, it's Dale who breaks the silence with what's most on his mind at the moment. "Why are you doing this?"

Doctor Hall is surprised at such a question. "It's what I do."

"No. I mean why are you being so friendly to me?"

"Ah, well...I'm not bound by the prejudices of the past, Dale. I'm the new kid on the block."

Dale puts the shaker down and just stares at it. Doctor Hall watches him. He wonders what horrors are in his mind. Will anyone ever know the truth? Is it possible that even Dale doesn't know the truth?

"I can't say I believe everything exactly the way you told it, Dale, but I have a hard time believing that you did away with Aslinn Perth in some fashion."

Dale's expression, if you can call it that, doesn't reveal much of how Dale feels about the doctor's statement, but he looks up at him. "Then what do you think happened?"

Doctor Hall sighs, pauses to look at Dale. "You were young...if some tragic event occurred then your mind may have dealt with it by transferring it into a more... acceptable version of non-reality."

"That's what the psychologist said then too...influenced by Welsh folklore and stories of Saint Collin."

Dale leans back in his chair, folds his arms and studies the doctor a moment.

"Do you believe in God...heaven and hell, angels and demons?"

Doctor Hall's brow rises, he nods.

"I believe in God, and...I suppose heaven and hell are full of angels and demons."

The teakettle whistles and Dale rises to fix the tea, but continues his conversation.

"I searched for answers to what happened to us for a long time." Dale brings the tea over and sets it down then takes his seat again. "Want to know what I think?"

Doctor Hall contemplates Dale, such an easy-going nature, someone he thinks he could call friend.

"Of course."

"The devil's influences are all around us now. He no longer needs to reveal himself to man. But that doesn't mean he doesn't exist -- or that he can't be seen if he chooses."

There's a knock at the kitchen door. They look over. It's Beth. They glance at each other in startled confusion. Doctor Hall pushes his chair back, "Perhaps I should --" but before he can move Dale goes to the door and opens it.

Beth stares at Dale. She wets her lips hesitantly and wrings her hands. Dale is so unprepared for this encounter again that he doesn't know what to do, but the doctor rises and calls out to her. "Beth, how are you?"

She glances over Dale's shoulder at the doctor then looks back at Dale again. Dale says the only thing he can think to. "Beth, I'm sorry about your...I promise you I had nothing to do with it."

How peculiar it seems that she wishes she could believe him. His face...so sweet, his eyes and his voice so tender...She wets her lips, "I..."

Dale steps aside, beckons her in.

"Please, come in."

The doctor offers her a seat and she takes it hesitantly.

"Can I offer you some tea?"

She shakes her head. The sound of his strong voice startles her each time she hears him speak. Perhaps it's just that she never expected to carry on conversation with the man who...She watches him intently as he sits down beside her and a shudder runs through her. Their gazes fix on each other.

The depth of tension is more than Doctor Hall can stand.

"Beth, I know what everyone is saying, but it is just possible that whoever is responsible is using Dale's arrival here as an opportunity to draw attention away from themselves."

They both glance at the doctor astounded.

"You should keep an open mind."

Beth glances between Dale and Doctor Hall, but her eyes drop as she answers. "Yes, I agree -- as difficult as it may seem. I don't want to rule out anything that might help bring my Lucy back to me."

Dale reaches his hand out to touch hers, but she yanks back and glares at him. Of, course it was the wrong thing to do. She's not ready for his compassion, she may have doubts but that's hardly an acquittal in her mind.

Beth holds her head down. It's obvious that this is difficult for her and harder still to look at him, but her eyes lift, "I want you to tell me."

"Tell you what?"

"Everything. About what happened to Aslinn...and anything -- anything at all about...", her head drops, she bites her lip, fights the tears.

"If you think it will help, I'll tell
you."

She looks up at him. Her expression is blank and
tired. Doctor Hall reaches into his bag, pulls out a small
bottle and holds it up.

"These are sedatives." He hands the bottle to Beth.
"Take one whenever you feel you need it, but no more
than one every six hours."

The doctor rises. "Thank you for the tea, Dale. I'll
be by later to check on your mother." He squeezes
Beth's shoulder. "Call me if you need anything."

She nods and neither one of them say anything as
Doctor Hall goes out the door. Beth looks down at the
bottle then puts it away in her jacket pocket.

"Where do you want to start?"

"How about on the Tor?"

Dale gawks. "You want to go up there?"

She nods.

"With me?"

She stares at him speechlessly, wets her lips
nervously and swallows. "If someone is trying to
duplicate earlier events, perhaps things may come to
you there that may help."

Dale's looks off as he speaks. "I haven't been there
since..."

Back to the Tor. It's the last place Dale expected to
find himself while here. In truth he meant not to take
himself very far away from this house, but as he
glances back into Beth's weary fearful face he realizes
that he must overcome his own fears for her sake as
well as his.

"All right, if you're sure? But I
don't know how it can help you now.

Behind the wheel of his Land Rover Dale curiously
contemplates Beth's decision to go to the Tor. What

does she really expect to find there -- a confession? He glances at her through the corner of his eye. She stares straight out and silently, nervously chews on her lip. He wonders, what would Aslinn look like now had she not...Dale's fingers tighten around the steering wheel.

He glances at Beth again. Her hair, though blonde was much darker than Aslinn's. She was smaller with more delicate features too. There were certainly resemblances, but yet they were very different.

Beth rolls down the window and lets the air move over her face. It lifts her hair and Dale thinks of Aslinn again. She knew the strength of her beauty. Her makeup was always perfect, her clothes neat and stylish. She even wore matching ribbons and bows on her clothes and in her hair. Aslinn was always on display for whoever was looking -- and there was always someone looking.

Beth, however, seems more relaxed in her faded jeans, lightweight sweater and slightly oversized jacket with the sleeves rolled up over her wrists. Her appearance is comfortable, he thinks, but her air surely isn't. How strange it is to be here with her like this, wanting to ask her questions, to know about her life, her family and yet...

A thud shakes Dale from his thoughts as a rock lands just inches from the windscreen and rolls onto the ground. Beth startles, shoots a wary glance at Dale for his reaction, but he just speeds up a bit and soon they're out of earshot of the rock throwing hecklers. He chuckles to himself and Beth stares. Dale looks at her.

"I was just thinking...here am I being accused of...well."

Beth catches her breath. Dale knows he has to be delicate.

"Well it's just that with all this trouble it seems silly to worry about a dent on the bonnet."

Without a word, Beth turns her expressionless face back out the window and begins to chew her lip again. She looks toward the West End Pub as they approach it. There are a few men leaning on a car in the car park outside.

Battersby, Brian and Ridley hang about. The men recognize Dale immediately. Brian is surprised to see a passenger in the car with him.

Ridley smacks his hand down on the car's bonnet, "There they go."

Brian shakes his head dumbfounded and continues to follow the car with his eyes. "Who's that with him?"

Battersby glares coldly then moves around to the driver's door of his car. Brian shakes his head. "Can't be, but blazes if it didn't look like Beth Bryce. He turns to get the reaction of his friends. "Ridley, John, you see that?"

Ridley opens the passenger door and the men look at each other and grin. Brian turns back to watch the car move up the street.

"But why would she be riding round with him?"

Brian turns around again to see the other two getting into the car. He knows the look on their faces and he is suddenly alarmed.

"You think he's going to do away with her too?"

Battersby shuts his door and starts the motor. Ridley holds the passenger door open and grumbles, "Shut up and get in, Brian."

Brian clams shut and gets in. He's pumped with excitement at being a hero as they prevent another Glastonbury murder. The car pulls out of the car park and takes off in the direction of the Tor.

At the car park below the Tor there are only a few cars left in the late afternoon and it's late in the holiday travel season too. The visitors at this time of year become fewer and less frequent.

Beth watches a family approach a car parked close by. Obviously on holiday, with travel brochures and cameras in hand, they debate over the next stop on their impending road trip. But it's the little girl that holds her attention. Long red braids bounce on her shoulders as she skips about the car park joyfully unconcerned with what the traffic will be like or when and where they will stop to eat.

Beth clutches her hand to her heart, closes her eyes and relives a similar moment in time with Lucy. She takes a deep, quiet breath and reaches for the door handle. It's only then that she notices that Dale has been still and quiet too. She glances over.

Dale's eyes stare up at the path that leads to the top of the Tor. His grip on the steering wheel is so tight his knuckles are white. He feels Beth's glance on him and abruptly releases his grip and opens the door.

Battersby, Brian and Ridley pull up in the car park just as the family pulls away. They watch from the car as Beth and Dale start up the path. Battersby pushes the switch that releases the catch on the boot and with a light thump the boot lid opens.

The men get out of the car and follow Battersby to the back of the car. Ridley opens the boot wide and Battersby reaches in emerging with the jack handle. He slips it under his coat and Ridley smiles approvingly and nods, but realization dawns on Brian in wide-eyed surprise. "Do you really think we'll need that?"

They ignore Brian's question and Ridley closes the boot. Brian follows their gaze up the Tor where Beth and Dale move up the ridge path and are met by a small group coming down.

Beth watches Dale warily as they move up the ridge. He takes in everything, every step of the way.

"It seems like only yesterday. You used to come up here with us." He turns to her, "Do you remember?"

She nods, "We'd pretend the Tor was our castle and the people of the town were our subjects."

He smiles. "I was the king and Aslinn was my ladylove and queen." He gives her a smirkish glance, "You were the princess, but you never seemed to feel slighted."

Beth's lip quivers; she clenches her hand in a fist, squeezes her eyes tight shut, then looks at Dale.

"Tell me about that day, Dale."

Dale stops and glances up the ridge. It was a memory all too vivid, not faded at all by time for it visited too often, both awake and sleeping.

They were seventeen and in love...he chases Aslinn up the sloping ridge of the Tor, tackles her and they fall into the brush and laugh...and kiss.

Beth follows as Dale continues up the ridge.

"The sun was just setting when we got here. Aslinn was running. I chased her."

He stops to look at the brush by the side. "I tackled her right here."

Beth is aghast, but he doesn't notice. He bends down, looks into the brush, sees the ivy and yanks a piece of it off.

"Then what happened, Dale?"

The light of memory is in his smile. "I kissed her."

For a moment Beth thinks how sweet and kind and gentle he seems, touched by a special memory. But, no -- those are false impressions emerging from her own memories and a time when she once adored him. Beth scowls in reprimand of herself. She has to remember what brought her here. She has to be strong for Lucy.

Dale stands and puts the ivy into his pocket and looks at her. He notices the displeasure in her face and realizes that this was a bad idea. There is nothing he can do to console her and likely nothing that would ever win her trust.

"What's the ivy for?"

"Souvenir."

"Legend says that ivy can help you escape from fairies."

Dale is surprised at her knowledge, but chooses to ignore it and starts back up the ridge.

"We decided to go to the top..." he turns to Beth, a glint of happiness in his eyes," ...to survey our kingdom."

He looks up the ridge.

"We hadn't either, not until that day. Everything seemed to change from that point on."

They reach the top. They're alone and Dale moves to the spot where he and Aslinn should have emerged from Annwn together. He stoops down, hangs his head and touches the spot with his hand and whispers, "I'm so sorry, Aslinn."

Beth's heart is beating so fast she thinks she might faint. "What are you sorry for Dale?"

His head rises, he looks out, but not at her. "For leaving her behind..."

Beth watches him warily as he stands. He turns to her. He wants so desperately for her to understand, to believe as only one other ever has.

"She was right with me. I had her hand. We were moving through the mist and I could hear the birds.

Then I heard voices calling our names...but when I came out of the mist I was here...and alone."

Dale pulls the ivy from his pocket, looks at it.

"This must have gotten caught in my clothes. I had the ivy...she drank the wine."

Dale can't read her expression, but he can't help wanting to share what he knows.

"I heard a hound last night."

At the mention of the hound Beth's eyes go wide. Dale closes his eyes, clenches his fist against the torment that wells inside him. He knows how crazy it all sounds, but only he knows too how real it all is. If only he could convince them. If only he could wake up from some terrible nightmare. If only he had never come back to Glastonbury. Why him? Why must Gwyn torment him? Why? Dale's torment expands in his lungs, tightening in his chest. He knows who took the children and he knows why. It's finally too much to bear and he lets loose a scream of agony.

Beth jumps back startled and frightened and when Dale opens his eyes he sees Beth's terrified expression and immediately regrets letting things get to him this way in front of her. He moves toward her slowly. "I'm sorry, I didn't mean to --", but Beth backs away. Her gaze is fixed behind Dale and as he starts to turn Ridley and Battersby pounce upon him.

John Battersby is not fighting in a blind rage any longer and with Ridley's help and surprise Dale struggles with difficulty to hold off their attack. Brian is startled by the suddenness of the attack and stands looking on stunned until Battersby yells angrily at him, "Grab him, Brian."

Brian waits for an opportunity and when they get Dale's back to him he jumps in. Dale is obviously no stranger to a fight for he uses tremendous skill with kicks and punches as he tries to fight them off, but when Battersby gets a blow in to Dale's arm with the jack handle the pain shoots up his arm and slows Dale down just enough for Brian and Ridley to get a firm hold on him while Battersby raises the jack handle again.

"No!" Beth screams in terrified horror at the realization of what she has become party to.

Battersby ignores her. He doesn't flinch, just holds the jack handle up threateningly. Dale struggles against the hold on him, but keeps his gaze on Battersby and the heavy tire iron.

"Where are the children?" Battersby yells at him.

"I haven't seen them."

Battersby lowers the jack handle and gives Ridley a nod. Ridley and Brian stand to Dale's side while keeping their hold on him. Battersby walks around Dale, pulls the jack handle back several times as if he were going to strike. Dale flinches with knowledge that he will and tries to follow him with his eyes, but Battersby moves behind him. Suddenly, Dale feels the sting of iron as it hits him behind his knees. Dale screams through clenched teeth and Brian steps back startled while Ridley shoves Dale letting him drop painfully to the ground.

Dale looks at Beth, but she cowers and turns away.

"What have you done with the children? Where's my Evie?" Battersby raises the jack up again.

Ridley grabs Dale's arms up behind his shoulders. The pain in his arms and legs is hard to bear and Dale looks up at Battersby in an anguished plea, even though he knows it's futile.

"I don't know anything about the children."

This time Battersby swings the jack handle into Dale's side. The pain is splitting and he can't hold the grunt of agony. His captor lets him go and he rolls to his side.

Beth runs up to Battersby. "Stop this, you'll kill him."

"You care?"

Beth stares at Battersby astonished and spins at the sound of the blow as Ridley kicks Dale in the chin.

"Tell us what you've done with the kiddies."

Dale grunts, spits blood from his mouth. His words are barely audible. "I haven't done anything with the children."

The sound of approaching voices stalls the next blow and they turn to see a small crowd of people rushing up the ridge toward them. Beth is relieved to have an end to the ghastly affair and rueful of her part in it. She had only thought the men were going to threaten him and while she knew Battersby well enough to think that it might come to blows she never expected anything like this to happen. Or was she just afraid to admit it?

The men back away from Dale and Battersby slips the tire iron under his coat as the people rush up to them and peruse the scene. One man goes over to Dale. He stoops down to look at his injuries and inquires how he received them. Dale glances up at Battersby and winces as he replies, "Just get me to the doctor."

The man glances up at Battersby, Ridley, Brian and Beth. "You sure that's all you want?" Dale winces as the man helps him to stand and nods then his eyes find Beth. She gazes at him ruefully and then quickly turns away. She wipes at tears and her shoulders heave in silent sobs.

Dale wipes at the blood on his face and grimaces in pain.

Doctor Hall finishes wrapping Dale's ribs and lifts his chin. He examines the bruise, then looks Dale square in the eye. "Still have all your teeth?"

Dale grins widely demonstrating he does. Doctor Hall smiles and moves to the medicine cabinet. On the shelf beside other well labeled medicines is a large clear bottle marked with masking tape. On it is written: HOLY WATER. The bottle is full.

Dale climbs off the exam table gingerly, favoring one leg. He puts his shirt on in stiff, slow movements and watches the doctor take pills from a large bottle and put them into a smaller one then he notices the bottle of water.

The doctor brings the pill bottle over and hands it to Dale. He takes it and looks at it.

"What's this for?"

"Pain."

Dale gives a nod of understanding, dispenses two into his hand, throws them into his mouth and swallows then he pockets the bottle and looks at the medicine cabinet while he finishes buttoning his shirt.

"What's with the holy water?"

Doctor Hall smirks. "A present from one of my patients. Out of the chalice well. No practice should be without it." Doctor Hall watches Dale start to tuck in his shirt and just the thought of the pain he must be feeling makes him grimace. The pain makes Dale think better of it too and he decides to leave his shirttail out.

Watching Dale and getting to know him makes it difficult for him to think of Dale as someone who could do the kinds of horrendous things for which he's been accused, but then he never expected such behavior out of Beth either and the thoughts give way to his voice. "I just can't believe Beth would set you up that way."

Dale puts his hand on the doctor's shoulder. "That's what I like about you doc, you have faith in people -- even me."

Dale picks up his jacket and Doctor Hall realizes that Dale is right, perhaps it's a character flaw, but he doesn't really think so. "What are you going to do?"

"I'm going to go home and visit with my mother."

Dale glances at the medicine cabinet as he starts for the door. "You use that water?"

"Never yet. Want some?"

"I wouldn't mind."

The doctor gazes surprised, but it occurs to him that whatever Dale is he is a most unusual man. He goes over and removes the bottle and a smaller empty container. He puts both containers on the counter and begins to remove the lid on the smaller one, but stops. He turns to look at Dale and then he grabs the large bottle, leaving the smaller one behind and goes over to Dale.

"I don't know if it works, but if it does you're the one who needs it most."

The doctor hands Dale the bottle. Dale looks from the bottle to the doctor and smiles then reaches for the doctor's hand.

"You have insight too, doc."

The doctor chuckles, there's just something about Dale that makes him feel warm. "Name's David."

"David, the shepherd who watches over his flock." The doctor smiles, but Dale's face becomes serious.

"Thanks for being my friend, David." He turns and starts out the door.

76

"Wait till you get my bill?"

Dale grins. With the door closed behind him he holds the bottle up and gazes into the clear water.

FATE OF ANGELS

Dale gazes into the bottle of holy water. The fall of evening and the earlier events on the Tor had finally brought some peace to the house and to avoid any further conflict Dale had made himself scarce while Mrs. Dewar served his mother's dinner. He waited until she left to scavenge the pantry and refrigerator for his own repast, which consisted of three fried eggs, some sausage and a blueberry scone. After finishing his meal, and washing and putting away the dishes, Dale gathered the tools of his journey and spread them out on the table before him. He set about first to pray and read a passage from the bible, an after dinner routine he'd followed for years, but this time instead of following his chronological order, which at present was in Timothy, he decided to read Psalms 23. Slowly he feels serenity ease into his tense, tired shoulders and he glances at the bottle of holy water again lying there with the ivy, a knapsack, two flasks and an empty iodine bottle.

His body aches and serves to remind him how lucky he'd been. Battersby could easily have broken more than a couple of ribs. If the other two men who held him had not been so close, he felt sure that the blows to his legs would have been more severe.

Dale rests his hand upon the worn cover of his bible. His eyes close and he sits there for a moment in quiet meditation. When he opens his eyes again he breathes a sigh of renewed strength and purpose and reaches for the empty iodine bottle, which he begins to fill with the holy water.

Doctor Hall locks the front door of the clinic and moves out of the bright illumination of the street lamp and into the dim light of the car park on the side of the building. As he approaches his car he notices someone stands nearby. With thoughts of what happened to Dale earlier and his involvement with Dale he begins to wonder that he may be a target too, but as he gets close he realizes that it's Beth. Having already felt the sting of her hand, he's not entirely relieved to see her, but then it occurs to him that she may have received some word and his apprehension gives way to compassion.

"Beth! Any word on Lucy or Evie?"

She looks down. Her voice is a whisper. "No."

Doctor Hall puts his hand on her arm. She looks up at him and the look in her eyes breaks his heart. There's no way he can know the kind of pain she must be feeling, but he knows it was an act of desperation that led her to set Dale up the way she did and all he can think of to say is, "I really am so sorry about all this."

She looks down. "I am too."

He watches her and wishes desperately there was something else he could do, but fear of having already done too much to help set recent events into motion make him reticent. Then just as he's about to make his excuses to get out of this uncomfortable situation, Beth looks up from her fiddling hands and says, "Are you going to Mrs. Conklin's now?"

"Yes, I'm just --"

"May I ride along with you?"

His eyebrows rise in question.

"I want to apologize for what happened earlier, but I'm just not comfortable going over there alone. I'm sure it makes no sense at all."

Doctor Hall opens the car door, puts his bag inside while he considers the implications.

"You're not convinced he's responsible."

Now it's she who looks surprised, but she sighs resignedly, "I think he's crazy, responsible or not. I think the whole world has gone crazy and me with it." Then Beth's emotions begin to overwhelm her again as tears well up in her eyes, "I'd do anything to get Lucy back."

He smiles compassionately and holds the door for her. "I'd be glad for the company."

Propped up against the pillows and feeling healthier and more alert than she has in some time, Mrs. Conklin gazes out the window at the familiar dark shadow of the Tor. She wonders if everyone in Glastonbury feels connected to it in some way. She always had, but then she'd felt that connection was even stronger in her son. He'd spent so much time there as a child.

A knock at her door brings her out of her thoughts and she watches Dale come to her with a wary look in his eyes. It's a look, she recalls, much like the one he had when he was twelve and he and Charles Castleberry had been skipping school.

It wasn't she who caught him, but Mr. Westmoreland, the history teacher. They had not known that class that day included a field trip to Glastonbury Abbey. She could imagine the surprise on the boys' faces when their entire history class greeted them as they rolled past on their way there. It had been part of his punishment to inform his mother that Mr. Westmoreland would be coming by later to discuss further punishment for their deed and he had approached her with the same wary look then. But this time she knew what it was about before he spoke it.

She turns her gaze back toward the Tor. She would not hide from it, though it gave her pain in her heart every time she saw it. It was responsible for the way they both had lived their lives -- in its shadow, always, but it would not be the last thing she'd see in life. She was determined that Dale's face would be her final gift.

She feels her weight shift as Dale sits on the edge of the bed. He follows her gaze to the Tor and she's the first to speak. "I heard all the stories too as a child growing up. Some of the same stories I told you." She chokes on tears. "Maybe that's why I've had you all these years."

Dale takes her hand. She turns her teary face towards him and he gazes at her lovingly and shakes his head.

"You know, don't you?"

She squeezes his hand and nods.

"You know I have to."

She nods again. This time the tears start to flow down her cheeks and it's more than Dale's heart can bear. He stifles his own tears. "I'm so sorry. I know I've let you down."

She puts her hand on his face. "It's I who have let you down."

Dale looks at her in astonishment. "How can you say that?" He takes her hand on his face and kisses it. "You have been my strength and inspiration. Without you...I can't bear to think what my life would have been like. You taught me to have faith in God and I have known power and strength to endure all of this because of it. You taught me compassion and exercised your faith through the most difficult times and taught me that all things are made right with God."

Tears stream down her face and he hugs her. "I love you, Mother."

"I love you too, Dale. You've always been a good son and I've always been so proud of you."

She gazes at him and her grip on him is strong. "And I'm proud of you now. I know the Lord has chosen you to this task and I put you in his care."

Dale hugs her again. He knows it may be the last chance he has to say goodbye and he's reluctant to let go. "What will I do without you?"

She pushes him back to look in his eyes, "It's not right for you to cling to me. I've been selfish and I'm sorry." Dale starts to object but she stops him, "You should get married, have a family."

"But no one else has ever believed in me the way you do."

She grabs his hand and presses it tight. "The Lord will find a way. He will not leave you alone or lonely. This is what I pray for now."

He smiles, kisses her cheek and whispers, "From your lips to God's ears." Then Dale takes the most reluctant steps he has ever had to and goes to the door.

She watches him go out then turns to look at the Tor.

Beth had decided to wait on the Conklin's front porch while Doctor Hall went inside to see to Mrs. Conklin and hopefully, create a portal for her to make amends. She wishes now she had waited in the car and wraps her arms around the shiver of the cold. She looks out at the shadowy figure of the Tor. The stars are bright against it in the sky. She wonders if Lucy is warm, but she sees visions of her huddled in a cold dark place, frightened and alone and reprimands herself for desiring comfort.

The frustration of all the nothingness makes her shivers more intense. There is nothing she can do, nothing but wait and waiting grows more difficult expectations with each passing minute. The sound of the kitchen door as it opens startles her out of her dark thoughts and Beth turns in anxious anticipation of seeing Dale, but Doctor Hall comes out with his bag and closes the door behind him.

"I'm not surprised they wouldn't see me."

Doctor Hall's brow creases in concern. "You said you thought Dale was crazy -- why?"

Beth wonders now if it wasn't a bad idea to have the doctor intercede in her behalf and what he may have had to endure. "Things he said, the way he acted." "Today -- when you were with him on the Tor?"

She nods and he stares out contemplatively before he turns his look back at her.

"She wouldn't say exactly, but I think she means he intends to go back there."

84

"Mrs. Conklin said Dale's going back to the Tor?"

Doctor Hall shakes his head. "I think she means Annwn."

Hounds bark in the distance and Beth turns toward the sound and shudders. Her voice is barely a whisper, "Gwyn's on the hunt."

Doctor Hall isn't sure he's understood her, "What?"

She turns back to the doctor. "It's what Dale meant today, I think, when he said he heard the hounds last night." She turns to look back into the night. "I heard them too. It's supposed to mean Gwyn's on the hunt for souls."

The eerie sounds of the hounds in the distance again break their stare. Doctor Hall grabs Beth's arm and pulls her along as he rushes to the car. "We have to get up there. There's no telling what he may be up to." Then Doctor Hall stops. He looks at Beth. "Perhaps you'd better stay here."

"No, I'm coming with you." He's about to disagree, but Beth gives him an obstinate glance. "I have to."

She opens the car door and Doctor Hall jogs around to the other side. Beth stares out at the Tor before getting in. She feels the pain of knowing her child is in desperate trouble, but she can't or won't dismiss the feeling that somehow Lucy will come back to her. She feels a desperation of her own too, to know the truth and not even the heat of the car's motor can still the shudder that runs through her. *How can I go in search of the truth and yet fear it so much?* The car jerks forward and Beth closes her eyes in a silent prayer. *Dear Lord, let your angles protect them and bring them back to us.*

The calm stillness of night so opposes Dale's disconcertedness that he feels as if he is in the eye of a hurricane, the momentary peace before a turbulent storm.

With his knapsack slung over one shoulder and a flashlight to lead his way, Dale climbs the ridge path. His inflamed nerves, intensified by agitation are aroused with every step.

Dale washes the flashlight over a thick patch of brush. This is the place he last held Aslinn in their passionate embrace, the place where earlier today, he took the ivy. He kneels delicately on his hurt leg and pushes through it using his hand and the flashlight until the light finds a large stone set into the hillside and sighs.

Dale slips the knapsack off his shoulder and sits close in the brush near the stone, keeping a tight grasp on the strap of the knapsack for it contained all the things he needed for survival on his journey into Annwn.

He closes his eyes against the pain of his wounds draws in a deep calming breath, but the hairs on his neck prickle and he opens them again alarmed by the bellow of a hound.

"I'm here, Gwyn."

Again, very close, the hound laments. A shiver runs through Dale, but he keeps his voice strong and steady. "Come on Gwyn, what's the matter? You couldn't take me as a boy so now you're afraid to try me as a man?"

"But I did take you -- I just didn't keep you."

Dale turns around in a start. His pain is replaced by an icy chill. He stands face to face with Gwyn, his hound by his side, eyes glowing red with unnatural intensity. The brush and rock have vanished into a large opening that appears to be the entrance into a dark cave.

Gwyn grins, "I did keep your ladylove Aslinn, though. Has it bothered you all these days...that she chose me over you?"

Dale rages toward him. Suddenly he's in a white mist.

He can't see, can't feel anything. It's as if he's falling through a cloud then...the haze begins to lift and it is just as it was before. He stands in Gwyn's royal court.

The tables are set with food and wine and the fairies dance in their silky refinery to a haunting melody.

"Is it just as you remember?"

Dale turns his gaze into Gwyn's smiling face. He fights the urge to pounce upon him and remove the impish smirk and it's just then that Dale realizes that his body feels wholly restored. He tests his suspicion and moves his injured leg. His movement is full and without hindrance of pain. He glances about.

"Where are the children?"

Gwyn sweeps his arm out. "We've set a feast just for you."

"Return the children to the Upper world, they don't belong here. You have no right to them."

Gwyn barks, "Who are you to make demands of me?" then he feigns sudden realization. "Oh, yes -- but you are the King of the Tor. Does that make you more powerful than I, King of the Fairies -- ruler of the Netherworld?"

Gwyn puts his hand to his chin in mock consideration. "Hmm, I think not. After all, I have the lady Aslinn."

Gwyn extends his arm and a hand takes his. Aslinn comes to his side.

Dale stares at her. She is exactly as she was at seventeen, still young and beautiful. He looks for recognition from her, but she doesn't even look at him, but gazes at Gwyn adoringly.

"Aslinn."

It's as if all the years that had passed were a dream and Dale wrestles with his emotions realizing he was thoroughly unprepared for what the sight of her would do to him. Dale stares in thoughtful remembrance and painful recognition of the one he couldn't save and watches Gwyn lead her into the dance.

He watches her smiling face and graceful body in the warm embrace of a demon. There had been restitution in saving souls from burning infernos, but never enough to wrest away the quilt of losing the soul of his sweet Aslinn in the pits of hell.

Dale tries to think, tries to plan what he should do, but he's lost in the conflicts of his past. Then a graceful figure comes up beside him. Her red hair cascades over her shoulder and the layered hues of red silk cling to her voluptuous body. She presses close, wraps her arms around his neck and gazes tauntingly at him with stark green eyes. His eyes are drawn to her full red lips in a strangely hypnotic way as she smiles and she speaks, "Dance with me, Dale."

He pulls his gaze away from her and feels his strength emerge again. Dale reaches up to his neck and pulls her arms down. He glares at her, "Gwyllion."

She smiles, moves her arms back around him. "You remember, how charming." She traces her finger down his cheek. "Have I captured your thoughts many times since you left? Has every woman you lusted after had my eyes, my lips," and she reaches up to kiss him.

88

"I remember you lied to me about how to get out of here."

The fairies have filled the space around them, dancing, drinking, eating and laughing. She strokes his hair with one hand while she moves the other over his shoulder and smiles coyly.

"No harm done, you managed well enough. Surely you cannot hold against me what is in my nature to do."

Gwyllion begins to lift the knapsack from his shoulder, but he pulls her arm down.

"Yes, Gwyllion, the mountain goddess who misleads travelers."

She smiles and bends as if to make a slight courtesy, but Dale holds on to her wrist. "I will forgive you -- if you tell me where the children are."

Gwyllion yanks her arm free and sets her lips into a pout then she reaches up again and lets her gaze follow her fingers in his hair as she traces down his face, neck, chest and stomach. She reaches around his waist and pulls herself close to him then reaches for the knapsack again with her other hand.

"Surely this must burden you, let me ease your burdens..." She gazes wantonly into his eyes, "...and give you comfort and..." she reaches up for a kiss. Dale pushes her away and rearranges the knapsack on his shoulder.

"It comforts me to keep it."

"A little wine perhaps, will put you in better spirits for pleasure."

Another fairy maiden snuggles up beside him and she too begins to run her fingers through his hair as she lifts a goblet to his mouth. He pushes it back, forcibly. The wine spills onto the floor.

Gwyllion throws her head back in laughter then takes the arm of a fairy man that passes and begins to dance. Dale pulls away from the other fairy maiden and moves through the dancers toward Aslinn and Gwyn. They gaze at each other like adoring lovers and don't seem to notice Dale's approach until Dale taps on Gwyn's shoulder. Gwyn turns with a look of surprise and displeasure.

"It appears the Tor King wishes to dance with my lady Aslinn."

Gwyn gives her hand to him and steps back allowing Dale to take Aslinn's hand. Had he really held this hand before? He looks into her eyes and although she still looks the same he knows she is very different. They began to dance and memory versus reality fight for a hold on his mind.

"Aslinn, do you remember me? It's Dale."

"Dale? Oh, Dale you've come to rescue me at last."

"Aslinn, I'm sorry it's been so long."

"But it has not been so long, although you have changed...Dale?"

He stares at her pitifully, guilt at having not had the courage to face this trial until now wretches his heart. "Forgive me Aslinn, it's been many years."

She glances at Gwyn who watches them intently then whispers to Dale. "We must be careful so he does not suspect."

Aslinn begins to pull Dale around in a spin, but Dale becomes wary.

"Aslinn."

"Shush, and do as I say, it will be easier this way."

Suddenly Dale begins to feel dizzy. The music echoes in his ears and seems to flow through him. Dale lets go of her and stands still. He tries to focus his eyes while letting the dizzy feeling pass.

Aslinn throws her head back and laughs at him. "Your journey has been long. You must be hungry, thirsty and very tired."

With Dale's head still swimming, he lets her lead him to the tables where he can sit down.

"You must eat, drink and rest."

She pours wine, lifts the glass to her lips and drinks then offers him the goblet. The dizziness isn't passing as quickly as Dale had hoped and he shakes his head and blinks. He knows now that the fairy dance is a way they cast their spells. The goblet is a blur so he sweeps his hand before him to push the goblet away.

"You know I can't. I would be lost here forever, like..."

Aslinn's eyes grow dark; she glowers at him and smiles wickedly, but Dale doesn't notice, everything is still a blur and he slumps back in his chair. The weight of the knapsack seems ten times as great so he slips it down into his lap.

Aslinn slithers across the table towards him and stares into his eyes. He tries to focus on Aslinn, but the flame of the candle before him is so bright it causes him to blink. The flame grows to such intensity that Aslinn's face seems captured in its aura and Dale is struck with her beauty. Scenes of their lives come back to him and his eyelids struggle to close with the weariness that tries to overtake him.

"I love you, Dale."

Her voice is soft and tender. He feels her touch on his face and he aches to hold her and kiss her, wanting to return her love. He's back on the Tor, that day, when his passions of love and hate overcame him.

"Aslinn..." He feels her close to him and he wants to pull her in. He reaches out and rises to hold her close and the knapsack falls to the floor in a thud.

Like awakening from a dream in the dark, Dale remembers he isn't seventeen any longer and she isn't his ladylove, although his heart may want it to be so and he whispers a painful prayer. "Forgive me, Lord."

There is a rustle of movement and Dale opens his eyes. Another fairy maiden dressed in layers of blue flowing silk comes up from behind him. She drapes her arm over his shoulder. "Come, let me take you where you can rest. You can search for the children later."

Dale looks over to Aslinn's empty chair and fights the fatigue that still wears on him. He grabs the maiden's arm.

"You know where the children are?" She stares at him silently and he yells, "Tell me!"

Two more fairy maidens come up to him. They lean around and over him as they reach for food and wine. They taunt him with the food, wine, caresses and kisses, but Dale resists them wearily for he can't let their lips find his, but the blue maiden puts her hands on his cheeks to try and capture his lips beneath hers forcibly while the others press in all around him. Dale draws a breath in silent prayer of strength and thrusts his arms out. The force of his thrust is greater than the strength he feels and they all jump back. Dale can see them all clearly now and he grabs the knapsack and rises to his feet to face them.

"I want to see the children."

But the maidens' just laugh then twirl each other about as they slip away into the dance.

Dale shakes from unrest at the nearness of his demise. So easily Aslinn had once again taken him to the edge. He leans against the table, tries to regain his composure and strength of will, but doubts crawl on him like an onslaught of creeping spiders.

He sits back down in the chair and leans heavily against the table. Dale gazes into the candle. The flame flickers.

The flashlight sweeps the ridge revealing the path, bringing back the horrible memory of the earlier events of the day.

Beth wants desperately to find herself waking in the brightness of day with Lucy safely at home knowing it was all just a terrible nightmare brought on by Dale's return to Glastonbury. But when she glimpses the broken brush in the flicker of the flashlight it forces her back into stark reality.

"Here! Shine the torch this way."

Doctor Hall complies and the light finds the trampled, broken brush again. Beth leans in to examine it more closely.

"What did you find?"

Beth touches the stone and when she brings her hand back it sweeps across ivy. She tears the ivy loose and stares at it in her hand.

Doctor Hall shines the light on her to see what she has found.

"It's just ground ivy."

"We were here earlier today." She looks up at him. "He pulled some of this ivy to take with him. He was planning even then to go back to Annwn."

"Because he took a piece of ivy?"

"It's said that ivy can help you escape. He must have been collecting this for his journey back in."

"What will holy water do?"

"Why do you ask?"

"I gave him water that came from the chalice well."

Beth stares in cognizant revelation then glances into the brush again.

"You know they also say that there is a gateway into Annwn on the Tor."

Doctor Hall points the light back up the path. "Come on, he must have gone to the top."

Beth slips the ivy in her pocket and they stride purposefully the rest of the way until they reach the top of the Tor. Beth can't explain the sense of knowing that they won't find Dale here anymore and she walks over to the spot where Dale was accosted and stares out thoughtfully while Doctor Hall walks in and around the tower and calls out Dale's name.

Beth stoops down and touches the ground there just as she had seen Dale do earlier that day. He said he had emerged here alone when he returned from Annwn.

"Could it be true?" She stands and gazes out at the lights of the town in the distance below. The only sound against the beating of her heart is Doctor Hall's voice as he continues to call out Dale's name and Beth considers the eeriness of quiet against the common night sounds.

There were many people that had had strange things happen to them here and she knows there were even a few who believed Dale's version of what happened because she once had too.

Doctor Hall sighs in frustration as he comes over to Beth. "Well, he's not here now, any idea where else he may have gone?" Beth doesn't seem to have heard him.

"Beth?"

She turns to him, a blank look on her face and instantly he feels regret for having brought her here. "I'm sorry, Beth. I shouldn't have dragged you up here.

You're exhausted. Have you taken any of the sedatives I gave you?"

"No."

He takes her arm. "Come along then, I'll take you home."

He starts to lead her away, but Beth holds still.

"What will you do?"

He looks at her curiously. "I'll continue to look for Dale and pray that no one else has gone missing."

"Then go. I think I want to stay here for a while. I can make my way home from here on foot."

He gawks, "Certainly not! I won't leave you here alone -- not with all that's been happening."

"Please doctor --"

"You should be home in bed and where news of Lucy can reach you."

She pulls a cell phone from her coat to demonstrate she's in reach of any news that might come. He looks at the phone then her. Exhaustion and worry have worn her physically and emotionally. It must also be wearing on her mentally.

"I'm still not leaving you here alone. If you want to stay, then I'll stay with you."

"I do appreciate your concern, really I do, but I'd like very much to be alone for a while."

"Then let me take you home."

She pleads with her eyes and he can't explain her desire to be alone here now except as he attributes to her current irrational thinking, but thinking it best not to disturb her further he hands her the flashlight.

"I'll wait for you in the car. Take as long as you wish, but I won't go any further."

Beth takes the flashlight from him and smiles wistfully. Then Doctor Hall removes the scarf from around his neck and hands it to her. He wants to tell her to be careful, but since he's examined the Tor thoroughly he knows that they are alone. Still he turns a worried glance back on her several times before reaching the ridge that will take him out of sight and back down the Tor.

Beth wraps the scarf around her. She lifts her chin up to the sky and gazes at a thousand stars all bright and twinkling in the velvet cloak of night.

"Oh, Lucy...I do have to try everything -- anything that might bring you back to me, don't I?" Beth swipes at the tears that brim in her eyes then turns the flashlight off and starts back down the ridge.

It doesn't occur to her that a glow of light illuminates the path helping her find the crumpled brush again and she snuggles close inside it.

"Ah, Beth you're a bloody fool." She sighs, then, "Gwyn ap Nudd do you hear me?"

The ridges begin to glow more brightly making Beth fully aware of it. She shudders and sits upright feeling the tension of fright from an unknown source then suddenly a bright blue ball of light comes at her slowly. Her breath halts as she stares and the light intensifies.

With the effects of the spell waning, Dale glances about for some clue as to where he should begin to search for the children when suddenly he notices everyone stands still and everything goes quiet. He turns to where the fairies watch a large bright blue ball of light form at the base of Gwyn's throne.

Gwyn grins and moves to stand before the light. Then he extends his hand and the light fades. Dale gasps in horror and screams, "NO!"

He runs over to her. "Beth!"

Beth gazes at Gwyn incredulously, but before

Gwyn can make his welcome, Dale grabs her and spins her around. Beth can only stare, unsure if this is some crazed dream or real. The implications are daunting and she grabs Dale's arm for support of her weakening knees and for something tangible to prove that she is not dreaming. Dale, however, is quite certain of this reality and he glowers at Gwyn with indignant condemnation.

"Send her back."

Beth's consciousness, suddenly absolute, screams out, "Dale! Where's Lucy?"

Hurt, anger and regret make his reply short-tempered, "I don't know. I haven't found them yet."

Gwyn bellows indignantly, "Enough! I am King." He sweeps his arms, "This -- is my domain and," he points to them, "you are my guests. I therefore must insist that you behave properly."

"Or what? You can't do anything to us unless we give in to your pleasures. It's me you're after and so I'm here. Now let her and the children return to the Upper world."

Gwyn glares at Dale and steps up close to him. "You dare to make demands of ME!"

Gwyn's words send a shudder through the stone castle walls like a low-intensity quake and all eyes fall upon him in horrified awe. All, that is, but Dale's, which raises Gwyn's ire even higher though he holds his voice lower.

"You think I have no power over you, Tor King? Think of this..." and Gwyn strikes Dale with a blow so hard that it knocks him back with a start several feet and scattered upon the floor.

Dale wipes the bloody gash on his face and glances up with a glint in his eye. He rushes at Gwyn with the vision of years of dreaming on the moment that he tears

Gwyn's throat apart, but Gwyn steps back before Dale can reach him and two guards move up to block his attack. Though they point their swords at Dale, he shows no sign of intimidation, instead he smirks and chides.

"King of the Fairies and he has to hide behind his royal guard for fear of the King of the Tor."

Gwyn's glare grows darkness in his eyes and a red glow of light surrounds him. His royal guards move aside and Dale pulls Beth from her startled gaze and moves her behind him.

Gwyn raises his arms from his side and as he does the glow erupts into flames that shoot up from his feet and rise up all around him. His voice reverberates, "You are but a mortal man."

"And you -- a demon, with all your power, fear me."

Beth stares at Dale horrified. This must be a dream for how could any man so brazenly taunt the devil and have no fear of his power?

Gwyn and Dale stare at each other wordlessly then Gwyn sneers, lowers his arms and the flames disappear. "I fear no mortal."

Dale takes a step forward. He feels Beth's tug on the back of his shirt, but ignores it. "Then prove it. I challenge you, Gwyn ap Nudd, Ruler of the Netherworld."

Gwyn looks Dale over and he laughs, "You challenge me? Hah! In what? A duel to the death?"

Dale keeps an obstinate stance and Gwyn slips his arms behind his back as he moves around Dale for an appraising examination of his mortal foe. Beth slips her arm around Dale's waist fearfully and he puts his arm around her and holds her close while Gwyn circles them in his perusing manner.

Gwyn comes full circle and stops close in front of Dale. He stares into Dale's eyes, but Dale doesn't flinch. He will not give Gwyn the satisfaction of showing any fear and he smiles at Gwyn, "If you think it so easy then why not accept?"

"And the stakes...are you willing to accept the consequences?"

"I am, if we take Aslinn and the children from this place and you leave the people of Glastonbury alone."

"You make demands that cannot possibly be met. Aslinn is my ladylove now and forever will be. So too the children are forever inhabitants of Annwn."

"I don't believe that."

"King of the Tor. That is a title you gave to yourself. You would have to prove yourself worthy before I could accept such a challenge."

"How?"

Gwyn grins, "Accompany me on a hunt. If you prove yourself an able huntsman..."

"All right."

Beth clutches Dale's arm, "No!"

Dale glances at her pleading face and back at Gwyn.

"No Dale, don't do this. We'll find a way. You did it before. You can't trust him. He's the master huntsman."

Gwyn smiles at her comment, but his gaze never leaves Dale's face. "When we return from the hunt and have feasted on its spoils and rested we shall meet in this challenge if you still desire.

Dale nods and Gwyn steps back. He raises his voice for all to hear. "But...should you lose..." He turns back to look at Dale, "...they will stay and only you will return and never be allowed through the gates of Annwn again as long as your soul remains righteous."

Beth gazes at Dale with anguish in her own soul. She had never allowed herself to follow her heart, but had let the hate of others consume her and blame him. Now, with a flood of understanding she watches Dale draw a slow breath and nod his acceptance of the terms.

They will stay and only you will return... If he could survive a lynching how would he survive with the knowledge of their fate? Can he defeat the demon, Gwyn? He must.

Doctor Hall, the Inspector and the two Constables wander about the Tor. They scrutinize their surroundings and search for clues in the dawning light.

The Inspector scratches his stubbly chin. "This is bloody irritating."

Doctor Hall is aghast. "Irritating? Four people go missing and you find that nothing more than irritating?"

The Inspector glances up at the doctor, "Without a bloody clue -- yes, I find that irritating." He mumbles to himself, "All this business about the king of the fairies...Annwn. Utter nonsense! You must have dozed off."

Doctor Hall glares, "I assure you -- again, that I was wide-awake. I waited for hours and when I came looking for her, she was nowhere to be found."

The Inspector mumbles, "Bloody irritating."

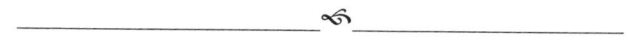

On their way at last to see the children Dale and Beth follow two fairies down a long dark corridor. Engrossed in their own thoughts it had been a silent journey disturbed only by the sound of their footsteps as they made their way there. Now, a cheery polyphony of flutes grows louder as they near a room with heavy ornately carved doors.

Dale knows that the Netherworld is not a place designed for children and although the fairies are young they are all beyond the age of reason. He thinks with certainty that the children could be returned to the upper world, but what if he should fail? He knows Gwyn can't be trusted to give him a fair fight and there is yet the hunt he must endure. If he must trade his soul and be trapped in Annwn forever then so be it, but he can't let Beth and the children remain here.

The fairies push open the large doors then take up their post on either side as Dale and Beth enter the room.

Bright light filters in from the many windows on the south wall and Beth gasps in relief when she sees Lucy and Evelyn holding hands and dancing with fairies in a playful circle to the flute music. She runs over and Lucy cries out, "Mummy!" and wraps her arms around her.

The flute players stop at Lucy's outcry and Beth smothers her in kisses, "Oh, my sweet baby."

Beth pulls back reluctantly to look Lucy over and takes Evelyn's hand. "Are you all right?" Beth doesn't wait for a reply, but grabs Evelyn up in her arms with Lucy and holds them both tightly. "Oh, my sweets, it's so good to see you."

"Did you bring Paddy with you?"

"I want to go home now, please."

The girls are clearly unaffected and speak as if they've been on some grand adventure, which has grown a little tired. Beth takes another long look at both girls and glances up at Dale. Aslinn stands beside him and Beth can't take her eyes off of her. She feels faint with shock.

Lucy tugs on her hand. "Yes, let's go home now, Mummy."

Beth turns her startled attention back to the girls. "Yes, we will go home," she looks at Dale, "we will all go home very soon."

Beth keeps a tight clasp of both girls' hands as she stands and stares again at Aslinn. Lucy stretches her hand out to her and Aslinn takes it.

"This is Aslinn. She's our friend." Then Lucy points to one of the flute players as he approaches Beth.

"And this is Aldren. He plays beautifully."

Aldren's strong build and height matches Dale's. His reddish brown hair, green eyes and broad smile form a handsome face. He keeps his gaze on Beth as he reaches for her hand, but Dale steps swiftly between them and pushes him back turning Aldren's smile into a cold glare. Dale holds his obstinate stance and Beth lets her glance move back to where Aslinn stands watching them with casual observance. It's more than Beth can stand.

"Aslinn...you're just the same...and I've grown older."

Beth leaves the girls beside Dale and goes to stand before Aslinn. Years of thoughts of this moment overwhelm her and she reaches her arms around Aslinn. Aslinn is non-responsive, however, and Beth pulls away to look at her.

"It's me -- Beth. Oh, how many times I've wished..."

It's as if Aslinn doesn't understand or care. She moves away from Beth, but smiles at the children, goes over to them then kneels down. Aslinn takes Evelyn's hand and strokes Lucy's hair. "What game shall we play now?"

Evelyn replies grumpily, "I'm tired of playing games. I want to go home."

"Yes, my mum is here and we must go now."

Aslinn glares at Beth, and then turns her smile back on the children. "But you cannot. There is much to be done yet and we have not finished our paintings." She leads them back to the easels set up near one of the windows and hands them each a brush.

Beth starts to go over, but Dale grabs her arm. "They're all right, but Aslinn is one of them now."

Beth gazes at Aslinn and Dale knows the shock and confusion must be very much like what he had felt upon first seeing her, but he knows also that simple mistakes come with great risk. He turns Beth toward him, "You must be very cautious of all the fairies."

Beth nods in understanding although her gaze never leaves Aslinn. "Yes, I know. I'll be careful, but..."

"If I can defeat Gwyn then perhaps we will all make it out of here, but whatever happens..." Beth turns her gaze on Dale. The tone of his voice concerns her and she sees worry in his dark eyes. "I will not allow you and the children to remain." He squeezes her hand. "I promise."

Beth wonders how Dale could make such a promise, but considering everything she now knows and everything she's seen, she believes it's a promise Dale means to keep.

Beth watches Aslinn with the girls at their easels. "She doesn't know me. How could she? I was only

Lucy's age when she..." Beth looks at Dale ruefully, touches his arm. "I'm so sorry, Dale...for everything."

Dale puts his hand on hers and smiles. "You think anyone will believe you?"

"We will get out of here, won't we...all of us?"

"Yes", he squeezes her hand. "I promise."

Aslinn and the girls squeal with delight at their easels. Although they toss their brushes wildly over the canvass, bright glittering colors form lovely paintings of butterflies that flutter and fly off the canvass. The girls skip around chasing the butterflies, but Aslinn spreads her arms and several come to light upon her silken sleeves. Lucy and Evelyn squeal with delight then mimic Aslinn and the butterflies settle upon their arms too. Lucy turns to Beth, "Look! Look, Mum!"

Beth turns a worried glance to Dale and he squeezes her hand again, "I'll do whatever it takes."

Aslinn's laughter dies abruptly as Gwyn grabs her in a firm embrace. He pulls her head back, kisses her neck, face and lips then looks at her sternly. "I am master of your heart?"

She whispers as she reaches hungrily for another kiss. "You and only you, Gwyn are my love and my lord."

"You care not what I do to him?"

Aslinn glowers, "He called himself a king, but it is you who gave me a crown. He thought he knew so much, but it was you who gave me knowledge."

Gwyn nods, satisfied, then pulls her close and kisses her again. Aslinn whispers in his ear. "You will bring his body back so that I may dance upon it."

Gwyn grins at her, "If that is my ladylove's desire." He spins her around and pulls her down to him on a seat near the window. "We will feast on the spoils of the hunt at his funeral."

Aslinn slips her fingers behind Gwyn's head and smiles. He returns a smile and then the sound of hooves clopping on stone pavement and the rattle of a wooden cart rises up from the grounds below.

The hunting troop, serfs and huntsmen, form in preparation for their journey at the castle gates.

Beth sits on the window seat of the play room and looks out onto the still dead view beyond the castle walls. The appearance reminds Beth of the lifeless, lusterless, drab cold of winter, but she thinks she will never think of it quite that way again. All colors are in faded hues. The brownish grass is almost transparent of color and gray trees arch with twisted branches toward a burnished red sky as if grasping at unforeseen objects. The sight gives her a chill that she doesn't fill in the lack of a crisp clean winter air.

Evelyn and Lucy play on the floor together with a fairy doll and as she turns her attention back to them she thinks of Aslinn.

Dale sits nearby and glances at the backs of the two guards that stand at either side of the open door. He holds the knapsack in his lap and eats from a bag of dried nuts and fruits. He offers the bag to Beth, but she shakes her head. "I've had enough. I am thirsty though."

Dale reaches for a flask and hands it to her. She looks at it curiously before drinking. "Is this the holy water Doctor Hall gave you?"

Dale is curious at how she knew of it, but he decides it's not important enough to ask. "No, but I will leave you some...food and drinking water too."

Reminded of his new and only friend in Glastonbury, Dale wonders now what David must be thinking. He wonders too how long they have been missing for he knows that time in the eternal plane of the Netherworld is greatly diminished. Dale seals the bag of food and pulls out the small vial of the holy water and sets them both down.

Beth takes another drink of water and hands him the flask before turning her gaze back to the lifeless scene through the window. "What an awful place. I can't stand the thought that Aslinn should be trapped here forever."

Dale glances about the room. He had not meant to share his fare, but now he must look for a container to put some of the drinking water in to leave for Beth and the girls. He goes to a table which has been set up with delicious looking meats, fruit, wine, bread and cheese. Even their essence produce flavor in his mouth that makes him swallow.

He reaches for one of the silver goblets beside the flask of wine and peers inside it. Although it appears empty he turns each one of them upside down and shakes them to be sure of it before he pours the water in.

As Beth watches him she thinks of her prayer for an angel to watch over the children and it occurs to her that Dale is the answer to that prayer...so fearless and wise and strong.

"Why must you go on this hunt?"

Dale comes back to where Beth sits and hands her the food and vial.

106

He instructs her, "This is the holy water. Keep it with you always." She puts the vial into her jacket to conceal it, but looks back up at him inquisitively not meaning to let him ignore her question.

Dale is afraid the answer may weaken her confidence in him, if indeed she has any, but he doesn't want to lie to her either.

"Gwyn means to destroy me and he expects that I won't return from the hunt." Beth's eyes go wide and he goes on. "After we've gone, use your earliest opportunity to escape with the children if you can. If you should meet Vitiris, he may help you, but be very wary at all times."

Beth nods in understanding and Dale takes her hand and peers into her wide fearful eyes. "I'm not sure of its effect when taken, but take some of the holy water. The children may not even need it, but give some to them too then each of you take a piece of this ivy." He pulls the ivy from his pocket.

"I have my own, you keep it."

He smiles proudly at her. "I showed you the way out on the way here, do you think you can find it again?"

She nods, "Why can't we just leave now?"

"This thing will never be done unless I can defeat Gwyn. Why do you think he stole the children? It's me he wants."

"But why, because you escaped him once before?"

"Perhaps that and...," Dale gazes at the children then back at Beth. "He has an enormous ego. Perhaps he didn't like someone else going round calling himself the King of the Tor." He sighs, glances down. "He took my queen...and now he means to dethrone me for good...one way or another."

Beth contemplates his words silently for a moment then goes to sit with the children. Evelyn looks up from her doll, "When will we go home? I miss my mum and pop."

Beth touches Evelyn's face and strokes Lucy's hair. She wishes she had the confidence she tries to express, but her fears eke in like a tide as she turns her gaze on Dale. "Soon, I hope, love...soon."

Hounds bark and Dale peers out the window. The mournful howls put new trepidation in Beth and her heart quickens. She ponders Dale's composure and leaves the girls again to go and sit beside him.

Practically, Dale says, "It won't be long now."

"Oh, Dale I'm so frightened of what may happen."

Dale wraps his arm around her. "He beat me once and took Aslinn from me, I have to do this if I'm to prevent him taking you and the children." He touches her face and gazes at her tenderly.

Beth is compelled with compassion and regret at his tenderness toward her when she had been so cold and vengeful toward him. She reaches her arm around him and lays her head against his shoulder. "All these years I hated you. Now I know and...," she looks up at him and she can't fight the emotion that brims tears in her eyes. "I adored you, you know."

He smiles at her. "Little Beth, you've become quite a woman." The children laugh and they glance over at them. "And with your own wee one."

Trumpets sound and Beth starts. Footsteps of a small procession in the hall can be heard approaching.

Dale rises and faces the door expectantly and Beth grabs the knapsack and stands beside him. She looks for a sign of what Dale is feeling as he watches the door and waits, but his countenance is resolute.

The children come to stand beside her and she reaches for Lucy's hand and grips it tightly. Dale takes the knapsack from her.

"What's going on, Mummy?"

Evelyn chimes in excitedly, "Sounds like a parade."

Beth shushes them and Gwyn's guards come to attention at the door. Gwyn saunters past with one of his huntsmen and approaches Dale with a gleeful grin.

"How I love to hunt. We will have such fun."

Beth takes Dale's hand and gazes up at him fearfully, "We will pray for you."

He turns to her and whispers, "Then my armor is strengthened," then he gazes at Gwyn confidently and squeezes Beth's hand.

THE HUNT

The ride from the castle through the countryside and into the forest of Annwn had been a grim adventure. The dismal barren landscape was depressing. Dale often saw skeletons along the way lying in torturous display with gaping jaws fashioned by their death screams. Then there were the occasional screams themselves which he heard in the distance and the howls and vicious gnawing of wolves close by as they moved into the forest.

No one but Dale and his nervous wild-eyed bay seemed to take any notice of it, but it sent hair-raising shudders up his neck and Dale silently recited The Lord's Prayer to calm his nerves while quietly following the hunting party.

As Dale watches the last huntsman's horse splash through the narrow creek and scurry up the steep slope on the other side, he tugs on the reins to bring his horse's muzzle out of the thirst quenching water to follow, but the horse whinnies and balks at crossing the creek.

Dale glares up at Gwyn, with his hunting entourage and the hounds on the pinnacle of the bank. His horse snorts and paws the ground as he digs his heels into its sides and Dale has to jerk on the reins of his mount to keep him from turning about.

Gwyn halts his horse and turns to watch Dale with his amused grin, which makes Dale certain that his mount was chosen for his skittishness; nevertheless he's determined not to let this dumb animal or Gwyn get the best of him and Dale yanks on the reigns again.

Then Gwyn yells out snidely, "Shall we erect a bridge?" and laughter rings out.

Dale peers up at Gwyn and he shifts in his saddle snuggly and points, "You could follow the cart path, but by now they would be well ahead of you...and these woods harbor many dangers."

Given what Dale has both seen and not seen and heard along the way, he considers this no option and so he gathers the reins up once again, glares at Gwyn then spins his horse around. With quick sharp jabs of his heels in the horse's side it lunges forward, jumps the creek and runs up the slope. Dale is just feeling his success when he notices the horse duck beneath a loop of tangled branches which have the ominous appearance of a noose and Dale feels it strike his throat before he is able to avoid it by leaning backwards and sideways. But as the horse continues to dig his hooves into the soft upward sloping ground Dale is unable to control his weight against the horse's jerking movements.

The branches brush against his back giving leverage to his already precarious position and Dale sees the ground coming all to near to his face. He stretches out his hand to break his fall as he slips out of the saddle, down the horse's rump and then tumbles down the steep bank toward the creek.

Dale's not certain if it's laughter or cheers he hears as he rolls through the dry leaves and jabbing sticks, but when he bumps to rest against a narrow birch he catches sight of Gwyn's leering eyes and it appears that Gwyn is not so pleased as disappointed.

The thought disturbs him as he pushes himself up and brushes the dirt and leaves from his clothes and while he takes stock of the fact that he appears to have avoided any injury, he wonders what lies ahead.

Dale keeps his eyes to the treacheries of the steep slope as he climbs it, in long strides, until he reaches the top.

A serf holds the reigns of his horse next to Gwyn and Dale looks up at him as he takes the reins. "Sorry, if I disappointed you."

"On the contrary, I'm quite pleased. I truly never expected the animal to cross with rider. I hope you will be equally adept in the hunt."

Dale mounts his horse and glances at the crossbows, swords and knives the entourage carries. He moves his horse in stride alongside Gwyn.

"You haven't said what we are hunting for."

Gwyn replies nonchalantly, "Boar," then urges his mount into a trot. Dale holds his mount back and considers it unhappily. *Boar!* What did he expect, dear, rabbit? He shakes his head then spurs his mount on to catch up.

The hounds begin to bark incessantly, acknowledging they're on to their prey and they run ahead of the entourage which moves quickly to go after the hounds. Dale follows behind at a gallop until he reaches them in a clearing.

A wild boar is trapped by the surrounding hounds and grunts and rams toward the dogs with its large tusks. The dogs snap, snarl and bark keeping the boar on the move, surrounded and confused.

Gwyn is smooth in his actions atop his still mount as he pulls his crossbow up, slips an arrow into the string and aims. He lets loose the arrow straight into the boar's heart with the precision of an expert. The fatal wound renders the animal grunting and staggering until it falls dead.

It's an impressive sight and gives Dale pause enough to think, *the master of the hunt has made his first kill*, then, *will I be next?*

The unison of cheers from the entourage breaks into Dale's thoughts. They feed Gwyn's enormous ego as if on cue and Gwyn grins and bows in the saddle with a flourish of satisfaction. Then as the serfs move in around the dead animal to prepare it to be loaded onto the cart Dale wonders if there would be such cheers if he should win the challenge match with Gwyn. Would they sing "ding dong the wicked old Gwyn is dead?" Probably not.

Gwyn dismounts to examine his kill. Carrying the crossbow, he indicates for Dale to follow him.

Dale had never been a hunter, preferring to leave the killing of whatever lay on his dinner plate to someone else. He thought animals like deer and quail part of nature's beauty, but the sight of this animal left a decidedly different impression.

"Disgusting looking creatures aren't they?"

Gwyn smiles at him. "He will look fine enough roasted." Gwyn indicates the crossbow. "Ever use one of these?"

"No, but I should like to give it a try."

Gwyn hands him the crossbow and an arrow and Dale examines it while he glances around for a target. Gwyn moves toward a tree at the edge of the clearing and points. "Why not try --" but when Gwyn turns he sees Dale with the crossbow up and pointed with his sight on him. Gwyn stands stark still with a glowing glare in his eyes while Dale lets loose the arrow. The arrow swooshes past Gwyn's head and finds its mark in the tree beside him.

Dale smiles broadly, more delighted with the result on Gwyn than his ability to hit his mark well. He puts down the crossbow and starts to Gwyn. "I think I've got the hang of it."

Gwyn glowers as he strides back to meet Dale and grabs the crossbow from him forcibly. "Yes, so it would seem."

Dale watches amused as Gwyn goes to his horse. He mounts then waves one of the huntsmen over to him.

"Give him your weapon." Then he turns a haughty glare on Dale, "You shall have the next kill." The huntsman walks over to Dale and gives him the crossbow and quiver. Dale examines them thoroughly before he slips them over his neck and shoulder. He wrestles with getting it to rest over the knapsack which he holds on to dearly and since it takes some time, Dale doesn't notice the hunt party has been preparing to leave. When he looks up it's just in time to see Gwyn spin his horse about and ride off with the others. The cart creaks and clangs as they take up the hind. Dale mounts his horse and spurs him into a canter to catch up.

The entourage moves along the dry road they had picked up soon after leaving the clearing. Gwyn had taken up his place at the front and had not been his usual jovial self since the episode with the crossbow. Dale thought it best not to push his luck or Gwyn much, too soon, for he was sure that Gwyn had more unpleasant plans for him. So he had chosen to ride at the end of the entourage and alone again.

The decision had seemed best at the start, but the dry road kicks up clouds of dust and since they had been riding this way for so long Dale was becoming more than a bit regretful. Both Dale and his horse have become covered in red dust making them blend together as if carved out of one solid piece of stone.

Dale swipes at his face again and spits the dirt from his dry dusty mouth. He looks up again at the clanking sound of hoof beats and the creak of the cart that carries the dead boar. It moves across the wooden planks of a bridge.

The hunting party waits for the cart to cross the narrow old bridge. It's obvious it will take a little time for crossing and Dale, grateful for the opportunity, halts his horse and slips the crossbow and knapsack off to take his water flask out. He swishes the water in his mouth and spits again before taking a long moistening drink, grateful for every cool wet drop that slides down his hot parched throat.

With the clanking cart now rattling softly on the road at the other side, Dale can hear the rushing water of a river below the bridge. It makes him ache for a refreshing, cleansing dip and he puts the flask back in his knapsack and secures it and the crossbow over his shoulders again.

When he looks up again the cart is beyond his view through the thick forest at the other side and Dale watches the others begin to move along both sides of the bridge. With hopefulness that he may find a way to the river's edge where his horse can drink and he at least can wash his face and hands, he urges his horse forward.

The hound's howls that come from the forest, however, indicate they are on to prey once again and Dale's hopefulness for a wash fades. He rides up to where Gwyn and two of his huntsmen wait for him.

When Dale pulls alongside he notices Gwyn seems in better spirits, but then he admonishes him, "Do not disappoint me." Then Gwyn and the huntsmen trot across the bridge ahead of him.

Dale urges his horse to the bridge, but the horse balks again. Dale gathers the reins up. He thinks about the crossing at the creek and considers that at least this time he should be able to maintain his seat. Dale kicks the horse firmly, and this time as the last, the horse bolts and runs at a full gallop through the center of the bridge.

Too late Dale realizes his mistake, for he sees each pound of hoof send rotting splinters of the center planks flying up and away. Why had he not noticed that they had clung to the edges?

Gwyn smirks and watches with delight as the boards crack beneath the horse's hooves and give way beneath them and Dale can hear the echo of Gwyn's reveling laughter as both he and horse plummet into the raging river below.

Dale hits the water alongside his horse. The frightened animal flails and kicks, barely missing Dale's head as they move swiftly through the fast current. Large rocks protrude from the white rushing water everywhere, but the current pulls Dale through the deep water and he keeps his feet up and tries to ride the current to safety.

Water splashes into Dale's eyes and mouth. It's difficult to breath and even harder to see and he feels his body twisting in the water then a jagged rock snags Dale's knapsack and holds him there. He flings the water from his face and tries to reach around to pull himself up on the rock, but the rushing water and his movement only accomplish separating Dale from his knapsack and Dale is caught in the current again.

Dale watches the horse struggle to find bottom down river then at last climb out at the river's edge. He glances behind and sees the knapsack slam into another large rock. It's held there by the current.

Gwyn watches delightfully from the high bank as Dale continues to be swept away in the current, but Dale flings himself toward the water's edge where the current is less strong and begins to swim toward the knapsack. Exhaustion begins to overtake him; he slows and tries to pull loose the crossbow and quiver, but he's thrust back into the fast water and a violent wave washes over and rolls him under.

Dale prays for strength and glimpses a bright spot of light that shines through the ripples from the water's surface between the rocks. He pushes himself toward the light and with each weary stroke comes closer to the light until he bursts from the water. Dale gasps for much deprived air, but his relief is short. A dead tree juts from the river's edge. Dale ducks back down into the water just in time to miss its tearing snag then suddenly he jerks back. The crossbow over Dale's shoulder has snagged a branch and its precarious snag holds Dale under.

He struggles to free the crossbow, but it holds tight to the limb. Dale wrestles to remove the crossbow, but his frantic twisting pulls the strap firmly around his neck in a choking hold. He desperately needs air and he prays again.

I know You haven't brought me this far to fail here. Suddenly, the crossbow works free of the log.

Dale shoots up and gasps for air. He's barely an arm's length from the knapsack. Dale holds onto the tree and reaches for it just as it washes to the side of the rock and begins to float away.

He lunges in the water with a strength he was sure was not there and grabs the knapsack by the clasp with one hand and another limb of the tree with the other. He pulls on the clasp to pull the knapsack toward him but as he does the clasp works loose, spilling the contents into the water. He watches as everything either floats or sinks out of sight.

Dejected and exhausted, Dale pulls himself up by the limb of the tree. The empty knapsack floats to the shore nearby.

Dale is surprised at the nearness of Gwyn's voice when he hears him say, "We will rest here for a time," and he looks to see Gwyn standing on the bank above the fallen tree. Dale crawls onto the shore where the serfs are already at work gathering dry sticks into a large pile. Purposefully, he keeps his gaze to the ground, not wanting to see that smirkish grin for knowing he'd want to remove it, but Gwyn won't be ignored. "Hunts are full of unpredictable dangers."

Dale is incensed and it shows in his glowering eyes, but before he has time to catch his breath in rebuttal Gwyn turns his horse around and allows a serf to take the reins while he dismounts.

Dale drops in exhaustion and rolls onto his back. *Hunts are full of unpredictable dangers.* Dale takes a deep breath to still his anger and as he closes his eyes he offers a prayer of thanks and asks that the hunt be brought to a quick end. Concerned for the loss of his knapsack and all the things it held to help protect him, his body tenses in anticipation.

The voices of the serfs and the soft padding of hoofs on the riverbank as they lead the horses to drink though reminds him that he has time to rest and Dale breathes deeply letting the air fill his lungs and his tired muscles begin to relax.

He listens to the fire crackle into life and sits up. It will be good to have a chance to dry his soaked clothes and shriveled skin, and the thought brings an amused smile to his lips. Only a few minutes ago he was miserably caked in dry dust. Now his renewed comfort brings him renewed faith. After all, the Lord knows his needs better than he and He will protect Dale as He did in the raging river.

Warmth flows through him and Dale walks over to the fire. With a smile and a peaceful heart he watches the flames lick the dry timber, sending ashes upward in the rising smoke as it crackles.

The newspaper in Doctor Hall's hands rustles as he turns the page to refold it. He glances over at Mrs. Conklin. She appears asleep and he rises quietly and reaches for his medical bag to leave, but she opens her eyes.

"Is that it?"

"I thought you were sleeping."

"I am tired."

"Then get some rest."

He starts toward the door and Mrs. Conklin looks out the window. "No more reporters hanging round?"

Doctor Hall turns. He is sympathetic, but he
120

knows there is little that he can do to give her encouragement. She's not the sort of woman who can be easily fooled, and he's learned that she respects someone who is straightforward and direct.

"It's been weeks. No news is good news and good news is no news."

Her voice has a crack of amusement that matches her twisted smile, "You don't think they're coming back."

His mouth opens, but he's left searching something to say. She turns her gaze back onto the Tor, "He was gone three days last time, but he said to him it was only minutes. I believe he'll bring them back."

He watches her in silence and wonders where she gets her faith and wishes that he could share in it for he had truly liked Dale. It was still difficult for him to accept what must surely be the truth. But be it by fairies or demons, he just couldn't believe people could just vanish from the earth.

She closes her eyes and whispers, "I believe in you, Dale."

Doctor Hall turns and walks down the stairs. His heart is heavy, having become quite attached to her in the last months while attending to her in her illness. He thought of Dale. Hadn't he seen the same softness in him that he had come to know in her? *A soft heart, strong mind and weak body,* he thinks, and wonders what it is that keeps her going when all his medical knowledge tells him she should have passed weeks ago. But David Hall had always believed in the human will and its effect on the ill. That was why he enjoyed a small practice.

He was fortunate, he knew, to be offered the position in hospital at Glasgow where he did his residency. The pay was fine and could have afforded him many comforts that practice in Glastonbury could not.

He lived in a drafty old house with an old furnace that gave him trouble as if on cue at every Christmas, the kitchen windows rattled in the wind and would leak water round the panes in a driving rain and he was still driving the car his father had passed down to him when he graduated.

But hospital residency, though necessary for his education in medicine, was just as significant in his determination of how he wanted to practice it. Hospital was such a cold environment. Patients were unsettled and disturbed, not wanting to be there and physicians and nursing staff were often so consumed by the busy administration of medicine that the spirits of the ill were easily overlooked.

He stops in the kitchen, looks at the teapot on the stove and remembers the tea he shared with Dale that day that Beth had come by. He thinks about the events that led up to it and shakes his head. Still, it seems to him that the stress of the recent accusations and her son's disappearance...but, he remembers, she is no ordinary woman and he can't dismiss the feeling that Dale was no ordinary man.

He opens the kitchen door and steps out onto the porch. The Tor captures his stare and Doctor Hall wonders aloud, "Are you there, Dale, battling Gwyn ap Nudd for the souls of those he's taken?" Then the most unusual of feelings overtakes him.

Though he can't explain it as a feeling or thought, it's as if he's received the answer, and it's not at all what he expected. It compels him to do something he's not prone to very often.

"Dear Heavenly Father, if it's true...bring them home."

The playroom is dark with the window shudders closed. The children had grown bored and tired and so had been put to sleep on pallets on the floor. Beth had grown weary too, mostly from concern and waiting. They had not had the opportunity for escape as Dale had hoped for since the guards had remained by the doors.

Beth had curled up on the window seat hoping that sleep would make the time pass more quickly until Dale's return. It was a futile attempt though for her thoughts would not give her rest.

She had to pin her hopes and trust on Dale and that hardly seemed fair. What if he should not survive the hunt as he thought Gwyn intended? Would Gwyn then release her and the children? Gwyn had said that if Dale should lose their challenge match that only he would return, but how could that be if she didn't give in to them? Dale had told her how to escape. Could she at some time make her way to the hall that led out with the children? Perhaps if she could find Vitiris...Her thoughts kept her tossing and always back to one thing, Dale must come back and he must win his fight against Gwyn.

A silent figure moves past the guards at the door and finds Beth in the darkness. He leans in close to her and whispers in a low soft voice, "My darling Beth."

She opens her eyes and wonders if in fact she hadn't dozed for how could she have been so unaware of his approach and she whispers his name, "Dale," and reaches out to him as he bends close and gently kisses her forehead.

She can't discern his features in the darkness, but her heart leaps knowing that Dale has returned. He touches her face and hair and Beth wraps her arms around his neck in relief.

"Oh, Dale you're back -- you're back. I was so worried and frightened." Her concern quickly goes to the children, for if she had slept might she not have been aware if they were taken. "The children!"

He holds her close. "They are sleeping and fine, but I am so tired. Let me lie down beside you and rest for a while." He lifts the cover and crawls in beside her.

Beth is stunned by his action, but she can't imagine what may have transpired in the time since he left. In her many fears, concerns and newfound feelings for Dale, she desires to have him near her.

He touches her face again. "You are so lovely. I could think of nothing but you while I was away." Again, Beth feels struck with alarm. He presses close to kiss her, but she pushes him back and scrambles to her feet in a panic.

Beth runs to the window and throws open the shutters. The light fills the room and Beth turns to see that Aldren stands before her.

"Do not be angry with me. I wanted only to be near you." He comes toward her, but Beth holds out a shaky hand against him.

"Don't come near me. Go away! Leave me alone." Her raised voice stirs the children and she runs to them, pulls them close and glares at Aldren. Lucy wipes the sleep from her eyes.

"Mum?"

She consoles Lucy in a hug she needs to console her own shaken nerves, "It's all right. Everything's all right."

Aldren starts toward them and Beth can't control her fear of him. "Dear God..." The words have their effect on Aldren. He stops in mid stride, his eyes burn red and a low hiss emanates from his mouth. Beth stares, startled and finishes her prayer, "Please bring Dale back and get us all out of this horrible place."

―――――――――――――∽―――――――――――――

Smoldering coals hiss and smoke rises up from the doused camp fire. Serfs fasten saddle girths for their riders, fill water flasks and tend to their many tasks as the hunting entourage prepares to move out of their temporary camp.

Dale is rested and dry from his ordeal in the river, but he worries about the nervous condition of his horse. He strokes his muzzle and talks to him soothingly, but wonders if it's even possible to command a rapport with the horse he had come to learn was called "Fool". *Riding a Fool and being led by the devil,* occurs to Dale as he puts his foot in the stirrup and swings himself up in the saddle.

The horse remains calm and Dale leans down to pat his neck, but when the horse stomps and shifts he notices that Gwyn rides up to stop alongside him and he thinks perhaps the horse is not such a fool after all. The same anxious feeling overwhelms him again.

"When will this hunt be over?"

Gwyn spurs his horse and their horses begin to walk side by side leading the entourage. "We plan a large feast for our celebration."

Dale notices Gwyn is back in good spirits again and wonders what else is in store for him.

"Celebration? Of what, my death?"

"You could always choose to stay and live -- so to speak. Enjoy the riches and pleasures of Annwn without ever knowing the pain of death."

"You agreed to a challenge."

"You agreed to a hunt."

"And yet you fear me so much that you plan to see me killed before we ever meet in challenge."

Gwyn pulls his horse to a stop. He glowers. His voice becomes a deep hollow low echo. "I fear no mortal least of all you Dale of Glastonbury."

Dale smirks. He knows Gwyn's weakness is his ego and plans to make use of it to his advantage at every turn. "Prove it then -- I dare you."

Gwyn grits his teeth. His eyes begin to burn in a red glow. Slowly he regains his demeanor. His eyes return to their normal dark color and the smile he so often wears reappears. "We will end the hunt when you have made a kill. Does that satisfy you?"

"I won't be satisfied until I've defeated you...but that will do for now."

Dale urges his horse into a canter and Gwyn glowers. His dark eyes glow red again as he watches Dale's back move further away from him. "You will not escape me again, petty king."

Music fills the playroom again and Aslinn's red dress swirls as she twirls around. She and three other fairies dance in a circle with the girls.

Beth watches from the window seat and although it concerns her that Lucy and Evelyn enjoy being so occupied by the fairies she can't deny that they seem completely unaffected and natural. She trusts Dale's belief that the children cannot be held here and she believes it also when her fears let her. So, she decided that it was best that they remain distracted, but she watches the dance from the window seat to keep an expectant watch for Dale's return.

Beth can feel Aldren's gaze on her while he plays his flute. Every time she looks his stare is on her. She pulls her feet up on the window seat and turns toward the window to escape meeting his uncomfortable gaze. The iodine bottle containing the holy water Dale left for her shifts in her pocket and she reaches her hand inside to clutch it. It sends her thoughts home again.

She wonders about Dale's mother. Beth had been feeling sorry for herself for so long for all the losses in her life. First Aslinn then Quinn, her capricious artist husband she had met in university and her parents. Now she suddenly felt selfish. Hadn't Dale's losses been even greater? Yet here he was sacrificing everything for people who had turned their backs on him, shunned him, even hated him. The twinge of pain and remorse in her heart brings a tear to her eye and she dabs at it with her free hand and squeezes her eyes tight while she clutches the bottle again.

Beth thinks about the trick Aldren played on her in the dark. Had she been so transparent in her newfound feelings for Dale that Aldren thought it would be so easy to fool her that way? She's sure she knows the answer and that makes her wonder if Dale had noticed it too, but no, he was consumed in his quest as he should be.

Beth shakes her head, rebuking herself. How could she think of such things now? Fear overwhelms her. Is she really so weak?

Beth pulls the iodine bottle out of her jacket and with her hand wrapped tightly around it holds it up close. She can't let her weakness be a hindrance to Dale. She looks at the bottle. Perhaps it can give her the added strength she needs. At the very least it will make her feel better. Beth unscrews the top and sips the holy water. She feels a tap on her shoulder and jumps. Nervously she recaps the bottle and turns.

Lucy stands there, "Come dance with us, Mum." Beth quickly slips the bottle back into her jacket pocket. Lucy tugs on her sleeve and pleads, "Please."

"No, love, I don't feel like dancing."

"Please Mum, please..." Lucy pleads and pulls on her hand.

Aslinn calls out to her, "Oh, yes, do dance with us, Beth." Beth gazes at Aslinn. It is the first time she has spoken to her.

Lucy continues to tug and pull on her. "Please..."

Having been so distraught and consumed by her own fears, Beth begins to realize that she has not been paying much attention to Lucy since they woke from their nap. Lucy's pleading eyes make her regretful for this and Beth rises and takes Lucy's hand. She lets Lucy lead her into the dance, for surely this can have no harm on her if it has done nothing to the children.

Beth takes Lucy and Evelyn's hands in the circle and begins to move somberly with the music. She watches Aslinn and it becomes difficult to take her eyes off her as she thinks of how much she herself has changed while Aslinn remains the same. Aslinn is so lovely as she swirls and sways in obvious delight to the cheerful notes of the flutes and just as Beth thinks how she wishes she could wake up and find herself and Aslinn at home in their parent's house she feels Lucy hand clutch and tug on hers.

The fairies begin to cross through the circle, each taking a partner by the hand and twirling them about. Aslinn takes Beth's hand and as she twirls her about she says, "Beth, sweet Beth. Sweet little Beth."

Did she finally know her? Had she always? Beth is suddenly more disturbed by that thought than when she thought Aslinn had not known her at all.

They change partners again and Beth is startled when Aldren slips his arm around her waist and spins her around and around. He spins her so quickly and his grip is so strong all she can do is hold on.

The room begins to spin and Beth falls into the dizzy spin. The music seems changed. No longer a light fluttery melody it is now muted and haunting. Again and again Aldren twirls her and she spins. She wants to stop, wants to scream at him to stop, but she can't find her voice. Everything becomes a blur of blue and red of the fairies silk and satin. It feels as if they have all closed in around her. Colors blend then fade into darkness and there is only the haunting rhythmic melody of the music.

The horses' hooves pound into the ground as they run behind the barking hounds and toward their cornered prey. Dale ducks a low branch at the edge of a small clearing and pulls his horse up to stop beside Gwyn.

The hounds have cornered an angry boar. It charges the hounds fiercely jabbing with its tusks, but the hounds keep at its hind, snipping and barking. Gwyn gazes at Dale then extends his arm to offer the kill.

"Once this is done we'll return to the castle?" Dale asks.

Gwyn nods and backs his horse leaving Dale alone with the hounds and the boar. Dale drops the reins to take up the crossbow and load the arrow. It was easier on two steady feet. Fool shifts and stomps nervously, spooked by the grunting boar and snarling hounds. But Dale considers his high perch a safer advantage and brings the crossbow up to aim.

Gwyn watches Dale fight to keep a steady aim and lifts a small silver whistle up to his lips. He blows on the silent whistle and the hounds bark, turn and run towards him. Their quick charge past Dale and Fool cause the already skittish horse to rear, sending Dale to the ground in a hard thump.

The boar charges and Dale scrambles to pick up the crossbow that lies on the ground beside him. He pulls another arrow from the quiver on his back, tries to reload the crossbow, but the boar is already upon him. Now it's all that Dale can do to fight the animal off. A sharp jab of pain runs through his arm and Dale knows his flesh has been torn by thick sharp tusks, but all he can see is the dirty coarse hair of the enraged animal.

Fool stomps around wildly and close to Dale and the boar. Dale struggles with all his might but flashes of white pain burn with each increasing injury from the grunting animal's tusks.

Dale's eyes focus on an arrow that lies on the ground. He reaches for the arrow, but his struggle with the boar moves him further away from it. The boar gouges Dale in the leg. Fool has lived up to his name being too foolish to flee and as he remains close to the fray, he rears, whinnies and stomps. Then Fool's hoof stomps on the end of the arrow sending the broken arrow sailing through the air at Dale's hand. Dale grabs it and rams it into the boar's throat.

Gwyn looks on with displeasure as the boar grunts, staggers and weakens. Dale grabs another arrow from the quiver on his shoulder and stabs the boar again. This time it falls and dies. Dale stumbles to his feet through a white hot haze of pain and gazes at Gwyn.
130

His shirt and pants are covered in blood, but slowly and oddly the pain begins to subside.

"You think you can provide me more challenge than that, Gwyn ap Nudd, Master of the hunt?"

Gwyn spins his horse around. His horse rears and charges at Dale. The horse comes to an abrupt stop in front of him and rears again with hooves flailing above Dale's head. Gwyn looms larger than life upon his horse with red glowing eyes and then he lets loose a hair curdling howl.

Dale backs away and falls to the ground. The horse's hooves come down at Dale's feet. Gwyn laughs. "King of the Tor! Soon you will be king no more." He spins his horse around and trots off.

Dale catches his breath and pulls himself up. Already the serfs are at work on the boar and preparing to take it to the cart.

Dale examines his bloody clothes and notices that already his wounds have begun to heal. The gashes in his flesh are closing.

Gwyn smirks and stares coolly from a distance, but Dale eyes remain fixed on Gwyn as he goes to his fool horse. The horse snorts and Dale notices the vapor of his breath as Gwyn pats his neck. Evening is approaching and the coolness in the air feels good against his skin. He takes the reins in his hands and mounts. A mist begins to rise.

A fog rolls in toward the townspeople gathered at the base of the Tor for the memorial. Mayor Meyer sits behind the podium where Pastor Welch gives eulogy and rolls the program in his palms nervously as he looks out at the encroaching fog. Although not unusual, it is unsettling on such an occasion and as others notice it they begin to fidget in their chairs and mumble to one another. Even John Battersby, he notices, though he holds his sniveling, sobbing wife close, has his attention drawn to the fog.

Mayor Meyer glances at his watch. It is approaching dusk, not a good combination with the fog given the circumstances, for whatever the people believed about the disappearances of Beth, Lucy, Evie and Dale Conklin, they all agreed on one thing - the mystique of their tor.

Pastor Welch takes his seat beside Mayor Meyer and although he had planned another lengthy speech and enjoyed such opportunities to do so, he decides it's best to get the service quickly over. He steps up to the podium and taps the microphone, which squeals and grabs the attention and quiet of the crowd. "Let us close this service to our beloved lost with a hymn.

Pastor Welch scrambles quickly back to his feet to stand beside him. People rise, glance at their bulletins and begin to sing.

Mounted on a low stand near the entrance to the Tor car park is a plague that reads:

IN LOVING MEMORY OF ALSINN PERTH, BETH PERTH BRYCE, LUCY BRYCE, EVELYN BATTERSBY.

Through the window of Mrs. Conklin's bedroom the Tor appears as an island in a sea of fog. She is weak and tired. Her only thoughts are of Dale and how she longs to see his face just one more time before a sleep from which she will never wake takes her. With the scrapbook she holds grasped in her frail hands she prays aloud, "Dear Heavenly Father, Bless Dale and give him strength to endure and overcome your

132

enemies. Let your humble soldier win the good fight and bring Beth, Lucy and Evelyn back home again...and," she sighs and clasps her hands together, "give him peace, joy and love in this world."

Her eyes are heavy for sleep and she lets them close. Her breath comes in a long sigh. Her hands go limp and one slips softly from the scrapbook to fall by her side.

Beth lies on a chaise, dressed in a silk dress of deep blue. Aldren takes Beth's hand as she begins to wake. He slips his hand gently behind her head and reaches for a goblet with the other then holds it to her lips. "Here my Beth, drink. It will make you feel better." Music begins and the fairies dance about playfully while they prepare for the feast. Gold and silver table settings glitter in the glow of lamplight and sweet smells of bread and fruit waft through the air.

Still in a foggy daze, Beth is sure it was Dale's voice that spoke to her. Aldren tips the goblet and she sips, but the taste is not water as she expects and her mouth twists in bitter response. He smiles and strokes her face with his hand. "My dear sweet Beth," and she slips into a blissful haze and smiles with thoughts of Dale's tender touch.

The girls are cranky and bored, left to themselves in the playroom. They tug on a fairy doll, fighting for possession of it.

Dale walks in just in time to see the tug of war take its toll on the hair of the doll, much of which is left in Lucy's hands when Evelyn yanks the doll out of her grasp.

"Aslinn gave it to me! Now look what you've done."

"She gave it to both of us. It's my turn." Lucy reaches for the doll and they tug on it again.

"It's mine!" Lucy shouts.

"Is not." Evelyn replies and pulls hard.

Dale's curiosity at why Beth would allow such bickering is settled when he notices Beth's clothes in a pile by the window seat. His heart sinks in fear and he kneels down between the girls.

"Lucy?"

Lucy glares at Evelyn and lets go her grasp with a tongue between her lips before she looks at Dale.

"Where's your mother, sweetheart?"

Evelyn sticks her tongue out at Lucy in return and puts the doll into pretend dance behind her back.

"She won't let me play with it, but Aslinn gave it to me."

Evelyn shoots around. "Did not. It's mine too."

Dale grabs Lucy's arm, impatient for an answer. "Lucy, forget about the doll. I'll get you one of your own. Just tell me where your mother is."

"She was very sleepy so Aldren took her somewhere to make her feel better."

Dale's head jerks around to stare at the pile of clothes. He ignores the bratty snipes as Evelyn taunts Lucy with the doll and goes over to examine Beth's clothes.

He picks up her jacket and rummages the pockets. He finds the small bottle of holy water, ivy and the sedatives Doctor Hall gave her. He puts the sedatives and water bottle in his pocket and goes back to the girls.

"I'm going to tell my mother you were mean to me when we get home and you won't be able to sleep over ever again."

"What makes you think I want to ever?"

Dale grabs them both by an arm and they stare up at him.

"You girls ready to go home now?"

Evelyn's hostility dissipates abruptly. "Oh yes, please."

"Mummy too?"

Dale hesitates not knowing what to say. He'd felt so certain that Beth would not allow herself to be influenced by the fairies, but he'd been gone so long. He concentrates on the iodine bottle while he unscrews the top, but his thoughts are of Aldren and his jaw tightens. "She and I will come along later." And he hopes that is true.

"I want you to do exactly what I ask. Will you?"

The seriousness of his tone and offer of home has made them forget their animosity and they stare at each other for a pact in truce and nod their heads in unison.

Dale smiles at them, but he's unconvinced of the lasting discipline of two eight-year-olds and admonishes them again. "If you don't do exactly what I tell you then you may have to stay here for a very long time."

They glance at each other again then Evelyn, looking very humble says, "Please sir, I want to go home."

Lucy chimes in, "Me too, I'm tired of this place."

Dale smiles and takes the dropper out of the bottle. "I want you to take this...medicine." The girls curl their noses. "It tastes just like water, I promise."

Evelyn watches Lucy take hers then Evelyn opens her mouth and allows Dale to squeeze out a few drops of the water on her tongue. Dale recaps the bottle and puts it into his pocket.

"We must become invisible..."

"Invisible? That's impossible." Lucy declares.

"If we let no one see us or hear us then we are. Do you understand?"

They nod and he smiles and takes their hands. Dale leads them to the door. There are no guards standing by now, but Dale leads the girls stealthily through the hall.

The sound of music and bustle of activity grow louder as they approach the royal banquet hall and Dale stretches his arm out to move the girls back against the wall while he peers out.

The hall he knows will lead them out runs parallel to this one at the other end of the banquet hall and there are many fairies busy at their activities that they must avoid to get there. He turns to the girls. "Invisible, remember. If you do very well, you will get a reward, okay."

They nod happily and Dale puts his finger to his lips then pulls the girls around the corner in a low crouch.

Boar is roasting in a large skewer in a huge fireplace attended by a fairy that turns it slowly by a crank at one end. All the fairies are gaily involved in their activities to prepare the feast.

Dale pulls Lucy and Evelyn in single file along the wall. They move unnoticed by the fairies that move about with trays of food and wine as they slip behind heavy wooden chairs set at a long dining table. Dale halts the girls abruptly when a fairy carrying a large bottle stops at the end of the table. He holds his breath and watches. The fairy stands very still and his eyes glance about, then when he feels sure no one is watching he hoists the bottle up for a long swig. The fairy brings the bottle down and sets it on the edge of the table near Dale's head in a loud thud that makes Dale start and his forehead bangs against the table in a thud. The fairy shifts his eyes about warily then quickly wipes his mouth with his sleeve, picks up the bottle and jauntily trots off.

Dale breathes a sigh of relief and rubs the sore spot on his head while he glances over at their next retreat. More obscure, this table is heavier, although smaller and with no chairs. Near to the fireplace of roasting boar, with large knives on top, it is a carving table where the cooked meat will be carved and chopped.

The two fairies at the fireplace stand at either end with their backs to it and Dale pulls the girls toward the carving table. Just then the fairies hoist the roasted boar from the fire. Dale scrambles with the girls to get beneath the table just as the fairies turn toward them.

He puts his finger to his lips to instruct the girls to be quiet and holds his breath again and prays. There is a large thud above their heads where the meat is dropped and immediately the fairies begin to carve it. They begin to chatter about the day's events and those yet to come and Dale becomes anxious about their ambiguous hiding place.

He looks up apprehensively then out toward the hall. They are so close that he curbs the urge to pull the girls along at a run. With only a few feet left to go he knows that running is his last option. Dale turns his attention back to the fairies at the table. He stares at their too close kneecaps and funny satin shoes when he notices a movement from the corner of his eye. Evelyn reaches her small hand up to the table.

A piece of meat has fallen near the edge and Evelyn stretches her tiny fingers up to grab it. Dale slaps her hand down.

"Ow!"

Dale puts his finger to his lips again, but the fairies have stopped their carving and chatter. Their silence makes him hold his breath again and he takes the children's hands as he prepares to bolt with them.

The fairies step back from the table and just as one begins to stoop for a look a voice breaks the silence behind them.

"My belly speaks for want of meat."

The fairies turn to see who has spoken and one of them replies. "Aye! It speaks to mine as well."

Dale glances around the table. He can hardly believe it. How is it he should have recognized a voice he had heard only once so long ago? Was it only by accident that he had saved them, or did Vitiris, the fairy who led him out then mean to help him again?

Vitiris faces the fairies at the table and keeps the others attention with lighthearted conversation. While their backs are to the table, Vitiris crosses his arms and gestures toward the hall with one pointing finger. Dale smiles for he now knows that indeed Vitiris means to keep the fairies attention away from them and so he pulls the girls out along the wall and once again they crouch and move quickly past the busy fairies and into the hall.

Quietly, they slip down the long hall more quickly now than before, for Dale's heart is beating fast with so many close calls and to be so near to getting the girls out of Annwn. They near the dark hall where no sconces are lit and Dale hears footsteps moving quickly behind them, but he doesn't look, he pulls the girls at a run. So close to the dark hall, his thoughts race, he has to get the girls out.

They move into the darkness and the girls slow, pulling on him. It's become pitch black and Dale feels along the wall to find his way when one of the girls starts to cry and then Lucy cries out terrified, "Stop! I'm scared. I can't see. I don't want to go any farther."

Dale knows now that it's Evelyn that's crying. "Lucy, do you still have Evelyn's hand?"

Her shaky voice, at the edge of tears replies, "Yes." The sound of footsteps comes nearer and Dale lets loose of Lucy's hand to pull the ivy from his pocket. Lucy squeals, "Don't leave us!" He feels her bump into his leg and he grabs her again.

"It's all right, I'm not going anywhere. He puts a piece of the ivy in her hand and reaches around to find Evelyn. "Hold on to this and don't let go. When you come out of this hall you will be on the Tor."

A torch shines brightly into the darkness and comes toward them. Dale backs them against the wall into the darkness and watches the fairy approach. He considers his next course of action. It's only one fairy and if he's quick he can take the fairy and use his torch to show the girls out, but the fairy stops.

Then the torch moves. It shines on his face and Dale sees that once again it is Vitiris. He breathes a sigh of relief and waits for Vitiris to approach.

The girls begin to calm with some light to see by and Vitiris holds the torch out to look at the girls. He sees that they each hold a piece of ivy and his eyes drift up to Dale.

"It is wise to leave while you can."

"Thank you for your help again, Vitiris, but you know I can't."

Vitiris smiles understandingly. He looks at the girls. "I will lead them out then."

Dale hesitates and stares at Vitiris. "Vitiris, god of wisdom and learning." Vitiris nods. "It seems to me that you have too much good in your heart to be forever doomed to this place."

"If only that were enough."

Dale stoops down and takes the girls hands.

Go with Vitiris. He'll light the way for you and show you out. When you get to the Tor run home right away.

"But my mum."

"You go with Evelyn. I'll bring your mum home soon."

Lucy stares up at him with uncertainty in her large eyes, but Dale cups her small face in his hand and reassures her with words he hopes will not be a lie, "I promise."

He rises and watches Vitiris lead the way for the girls down the long dark hall, leaving him in growing darkness, then a thought occurs to him and he calls out, "Lucy!"

She turns.

"Tell Doctor Hall that Dale says thanks for the water."

"Yes, sir."

He watches them slip into a thick mist until he can no longer see them. His relief in knowing the children will make it safely home is short though for his thoughts go immediately to Beth and the final challenge with Gwyn. How did the fates of so many people wind up in his hands?

THE TRUE KING

Steam rises from a thick pot of stew. The tables are covered with pots of stews made of boar's meat, sliced meat and delicious looking trays of food of all kinds.

Dale strides into the room with an air of confidence. He glances around for Gwyn, but finds Aldren instead, dancing with Beth wrapped dreamily in his arms.

A tide of remembrance rushes in on him. Aslinn had danced in Gwyn's arms in just such a way and he had lost her. Anger overcomes him. It cannot happen again. He will not let Beth be lost in the same way. It can't be too late.

Dale tears through the dancers, pushing them abruptly aside until he reaches Beth. He pulls her away and pushes Aldren back, glaring at him through gritted teeth, but Aldren only glances at Dale before turning his gaze on Beth with a smug smile.

Dale will not let himself believe that Beth is already lost. He turns to her, looks into her dazed eyes. His mind fights his heart and Dale grabs her by both arms and shakes her. "Beth! Beth!"

She gazes at him and it's a look that is all too familiar. Dale knows she's entranced. It's just as it was with Aslinn so very long ago. Every muscle in his body goes tight and it's just like it was that time with her on the Tor, but he fights the urge to scream. Then something seems to change in her gaze.

Dale sees a glistening in her eye. Is it recognition, he wonders or just a trick of flickering candle light? Then softly she speaks, "Dale."

"Yes." His heart leaps with hope. Her body goes limp and Dale pulls her to him in a tight embrace and lifts her up.

He glares again at Aldren who glares back and smiles. "She's mine now."

That's the last straw. Dale gently lowers Beth into a nearby chair and turns another cold glare at Aldren before he charges him.

The men are of equal size, but Dale's adrenalin is fueled by anger. When he throws his weight against Aldren both men sprawl on the floor knocking fairies into each other and spilling chairs and goblets of wine.

The fray is a delightful spectacle to the fairies. They cheer and laugh as they form a circle to watch the fight. The music stops and they chant, *"Aldren! Aldren! Aldren!"* to urge Aldren on.

Aldren and Dale are back on their feet again quickly facing each other in fighting stance. Dale delivers a fist to put in Aldren's face, but Aldren agilely ducks and slams Dale in the gut with his head. Dale manages to grab a fistful of Aldren's silk shirt and pulls Aldren with him as he staggers and falls until the fabric gives way. Then Dale rolls over and both men are up on their feet again, but it's Aldren who charges next and he slams Dale into the carving table.

Pressed tight against the table in a strangle hold, Dale catches sight of glinting silver over his shoulder. Aldren's red eyes burn into him and his face contorts hideously revealing gnarling teeth making Aldren appear more animal than man.

Dale is desperate for air. He reaches behind him. His hand must find what his eyes cannot. Things begin to blur in shades of black and white as his oxygen deprived body begins to slip into deaths grip, then Dale feels something cold on his fingertips. It is the steel blade of the carving knife. Dale's fingers walk over the blade pulling it closer to his palm. He feels faint darkness overcoming him, but he pulls the knife up and sends it to its mark with one swift thrust.

Aldren hisses at the stab to his heart. His eyes grow black. His hold around Dale's neck slips and Aldren drops to the floor.

Dale gasps air into his lungs and holds on to the table. He braces himself there to recover from his near death experience while the fairies stare silently at Aldren's limp body. Then their glaring red eyes focus on Dale and they emit a low unison hiss.

The sound seems to create a white smoke and Dale stares in wonder until he notices that the smoke rises from Aldren's lifeless form. Flames shoot up around him then build and quickly intensify until Aldren's body is completely engulfed. Dale stares, in only moments the flames disappear leaving nothing but a pile of ash on the floor.

When he brings his eyes back up to the silent, still crowd of fairies, one moves slowly towards him. It is Aslinn. She leers as she comes to stop in front of him then without warning she claws his face and snarls. "It is you who should be dead."

She tries to claw at him again, but Dale backs to the wall. "You blame me for leaving you here."

She hisses, "Yes!"

"I tried, you know."

"Not hard enough!" She moves toward Dale again and he doesn't try to stop her.

He knows that it's useless to try to explain and he knows that it was her own vanity that trapped her here. Suddenly the weight of years of guilt lifts from his shoulders.

Aslinn comes close; his eyes are fixed on hers as she speaks. "See what you left me with."

Dale's eyes become fixed in Aslinn's eyes and they begin to glow in silver light. Her eyes become as mirrors and Dale sees everything before her in reflection through her eyes.

The fairies are hideous and ugly. Their clothing is tattered, dirty and singed. The food is rotting, spoiled and crawling with insects. Dale shudders and turns away from the horror of this vision though he knows it to be true.

"I'm sorry, Aslinn. I'm so sorry." He turns back to her. "Help us, it's not too late..."

She laughs, "It is too late for me. I gave in to temptation and lost my soul. The only thing left to give me pleasure now is to capture yours...," she glances at Beth still slumped in the chair dazed and bewildered, "as I have hers."

Dale looks at Beth and his gaze moves beyond her to where Gwyn stands with a snide grin. Dale rushes toward Gwyn. "No! You have me! Release her."

Gwyn is nonchalant, "We are each responsible for our own soul."

Dale seethes, "A coward and a liar. You tricked her. Beth would not have given in."

"I have not changed the bargain -- only certain conditions have changed. You have released the children and Beth has become one of us. Do you not wish to honor the rest of our bargain?"

Dale staggers dejected. "What's left to bargain for but my soul?"

Have you forgotten the good people of Glastonbury? Is not a king responsible for his people?"

Dale gazes at Gwyn. "How can I trust you when you've not once kept your word?"

"Not true!" Gwyn snaps. "Perhaps I am not fully trustworthy, but that is my nature and something you should know. But a bargain is a bargain. And you alone, Dale of Glastonbury, King of the Tor, can decide the fate of the people of Glastonbury."

Dale rubs his forehead, shakes his head. He glances at Beth and tries to understand. Is it useless to try, will everything Gwyn says be a lie? "No," is the answer in his head.

My Lord would not have brought me so far to endure all this if there were no possibility of a good end.

"Perhaps when Lucy is older...," Gwyn chides.

"No! I accept the challenge and I will destroy you. Gwyn ap Nudd."

Gwyn smiles, amused and pleased. "I thought perhaps Aldren would deprive me of the chance to do battle with you. I am glad he did not for I have enjoyed no challenge as great as yours in centuries." He picks up a goblet, holds it high and looks out into the crowd. "To the challenge between two kings!"

Goblets rise in toast and the fairies cheer. Dale stares as they drink from their silver goblets and again he prays.

The teakettle whistles and Agnes Dewar removes it from the stove. She pours the water into a teapot then pours some into a cup and stirs until it turns a smooth frothy brown. Then she takes the cup of hot chocolate to the table and sets it down. Lucy wraps her hands around the cup excitedly.

Agnes snaps, "Sip it carefully now it's hot."

Lucy looks into the cup disappointedly. "No whipping cream?"

"Oh, I forgot. I picked some up special for you today." Mrs. Dewar smiles at Lucy and goes to get the whip cream from the refrigerator. She plops a large dollop into Lucy's cup.

"I wish my mum would come home soon."

Agnes pats her hand, "If Dale promised to bring her back...then I'm sure he will do his best to bring her back soon, dear." She turns to carry the whip cream back to the refrigerator, but stops to glance out the kitchen window toward the stark figure of the Tor and bites her lip, "They will both be back home very soon, you'll see."

Lucy leans her face down to the cup and sips at the whip cream that brims the cup of hot chocolate and Mrs. Dewar smiles.

It had been difficult to believe the stories the children had told when they first arrived, but eventually it became the only way to explain the mystery and it was linked to the past. Now, suddenly, there were many in Glastonbury who claimed to have always *had a feeling* or *knew...something*.

Everyone who had ever had an unusual experience there or knew someone who had, had been recounting their strange tales. Everyone talked about it and there were few left who didn't believe anymore and Dale and Beth had become a constant in the thoughts and prayers of everyone who did.

Agnes and Doctor Hall had taken over looking after Lucy though it was a responsibility that fell more on her than him, but she didn't mind. Agnes adored children and with her own two grown and away she enjoyed having a little one around again.

Agnes thought that the good Doctor had too many other things to worry about anyway. He now spent many evenings over at the Conklin house taking care of Mrs. Conklin, for her condition had once again worsened and she still refused hospital. She knew also though that his presence here was partly due to his constant hopeful anticipation of Dale's return.

His anxiousness spurred hers, especially in light of having Lucy. They spent the evenings at Mrs. Conklin's house and she cooked for them and they kept each other company while they waited. Agnes hated to think what would happen to Lucy if Beth shouldn't return and wonders how long they will be able to wait before some decision has to be made.

She turns away from her sad thoughts and goes to prepare the tea. The good Doctor will be wanting some soon and so does she.

Doctor Hall stands at the window in Mrs. Conklin's bedroom and looks out at the Tor. His faith in his ability to judge a human heart had been restored with the children's return and his faith in the Lord had been renewed last Sunday in church when he, like many others, answered the invitation at the end of the service. *David, the good shepherd,* Dale had called him, but Dale was the one slaying the giant and he prayed fervently for his safe return.

Doctor Hall turns his gaze back to the unconscious form of Mrs. Conklin. She should know that they all believe in Dale now the way she always had and it saddens him to think she may not be aware. They say the hearing is the last thing to go. If she has heard him, has she also understood him?

He moves to the chair beside her bed and sits to take her hand in his. "Just a little longer, hold on dear, Dale will come."

It had been a strange world for him since the children returned, and for most, he conjectures. Of course, there were some who felt the children's stories were cleverly contrived. *They were hypnotized,* or *brainwashed.* But David Hall listened to his heart. When Lucy had said that Dale thanked him for the holy water, he knew. Knew in his heart of hearts and he thought often of what Dale had said to him. *Do you believe in heaven and hell, angels and demons?*

He believed now with an understanding that he had never before possessed. Tabloids on newsstands with their large print declaring UFO's and aliens took on new meaning in his heart.

He thought of Dale, not as a prophet, but as a man whose purpose in life had been clearly planned. How many people now understood the overreaching power of the devil on this earth? Of course, he knew, some would quickly forget or set aside this powerful lesson that Dale had brought to them, but he would not.

He glances back at the Tor in the distance and whispers, "Dale's coming home. We all know it now and we're all praying for him..." he glances back at Mrs. Conklin, "and you."

❦

In the center of the castle's outer courtyard a low circular stone wall juts up to the height of about three feet. It appears to be a well, but within the deep pit, instead of water, flames spit and spew from the boiling molten bed far below.

The fairies sit around the perimeter walls engaged in excited chatter as they await the beginning of the challenge match between the two kings. The death of Aldren had not dampened their frivolity at the feast for very long and perhaps only helped to enhance their desire to see their king destroy the righteous so-called King of the Tor.

Two guards escort Dale out into the center courtyard and the crowd begins to hiss. Dale surveys the courtyard then notices the small table with two wine filled goblets at one end. He glances back among the spectators. Beth is there; front and center, probably to help induce his anger and despair. He goes over to her, kneels at her feet and takes both of her hands in his.

Dale holds the sedative bottle in one hand. He looks up at her face. Her eyes give him the recognition he desires and he smiles. "I won't leave you here."

Dale removes several capsules from the bottle and puts them in his hand. He slips the bottle into his pocket and pulls the iodine bottle out and starts to uncap it. The fairy spectators begin to cheer and Dale turns to see exactly what he expects.

Gwyn makes a grand entrance with Aslinn. He waves and bows to their cheers and leads Aslinn regally, hands clasped high, to the wine table.

Dale glances back at Beth. He must somehow get her to drink the water and hope that it will help, but the two guards start toward him and come to stand behind him. Dale looks into Beth's eyes. He's sure she recognizes him, but there's no chance now that he can give her the holy water so he puts the bottle into her hand, closing her fingers around it. Beth's other hand moves to cover the first and Dale stares into her eyes and is filled with confidence that her soul is not yet lost. The guards nudge Dale and he rises. His heart quickens as he goes to face Gwyn in his final challenge.

The guards escort Dale over to stand behind Gwyn and Aslinn and Gwyn gestures to the crowd, smiling broadly, and waits until their cheers subside. "My dear children of Annwn, today you witness a rare event. St. Collin was a wise man..." He gestures to Dale and Dale moves toward them. "But Dale of Glastonbury is more than that -- he is noble and brave in a time when men of the upper world fear to be good, lest it make them seem weak."

Gwyn grabs Dale's shoulder in an affectionate grasp and brings him to stand beside him. "See you this day, a righteous man give his life and soul for those who despise him."

The fairies cheer. Gwyn and Aslinn gleam with delight and he takes her hand and leads her forward. They take sweeping bows and curtsies turning toward the many spectators so as to acknowledge them all.

Dale steps back to let Gwyn and Aslinn revel in their glory and breaks open the capsules in his hand. He slips the powder into one of the goblets and just as he is about to do the same to the other Gwyn gestures again and the cheers subside. He turns to Dale. "Have you anything to say, Tor King. We'd be most pleased."

150

Dale closes his palm and steps around to address the crowd.

"What Gwyn has said is true. But he has failed to mention this..." Dale looks at Beth. "The righteous are given the strength and power to overcome all things. In Christ's name, I will defeat you."

Hisses rise from every fairy voice at the mention of the Lord's name and Dale turns to Gwyn.

Gwyn smiles, reaches for the two goblets. Gwyn raises the goblet with the sedative and hands it to Aslinn. Dale watches Aslinn and Gwyn raise their goblets to the cheers of the crowd and drink. Perhaps it would have had no effect on Gwyn, he thinks, but it was worth the effort to try.

He watches Gwyn replace their goblets on the table and turn back to the crowd. "Let the challenge begin."

Aslinn slips into the crowd while the fairies cheer again and two serfs carrying swords move forward to present them to Gwyn and Dale.

Dale hesitates as he reaches for the sword. Gwyn smirks, "It occurs to me that you have had a very long day. If you wish we could stay our challenge 'til the morrow. Perhaps by then your Lord could give you the instruction you need to master one of these, if you ask?"

Dale takes up the sword. "It occurs to me that since I've been here you've had no concern to give me any good vantage. I'd like to get home while there are still people there I remember."

Dale looks at the sword and a smile comes to his lips. He thinks back to when he was in training as a firefighter and first met Oscar Whorley. They had become good friends while in training together and Oscar had introduced him to the art of fencing.

Dale gives a brief prayer of thanks for Oscar and for preparing him for this journey. He holds up the weapon. It is of ancient construction, made of heavy steel with a large ornate coquille. Although very dissimilar to the lightweight fencing foil he'd learned the sport with, Dale demonstrates his familiarity with it with a parry and a thrust and smiles at Gwyn, "Your choice of weapons suits me for my Lord prepared me long before you or I knew of this day."

Gwyn gestures for them to move out into the courtyard and they face each other. As they go through the formalities that begin their match, Beth's eyes fix on Dale. Although she has all the appearances of being entranced and is truly without all her functions, her mind is yet free. The swords clash and Beth prays. Her hands clench tightly around the iodine bottle.

Dale and Gwyn move around the courtyard in a demonstration of seemingly equal strength, skill and close calls, which bring cheers to Gwyn and boos to Dale respective of which appears to have the upper hand at any moment.

Dale is sure that Gwyn is not giving his all to the match yet as he taunts him with many feints, but he's grateful for the opportunity to reacquaint himself with the sport and the weight of his weapon.

Gwyn thrust and Dale successfully volts, but then Gwyn's blade strikes the back of Dale's left hand in a searing slice.

Dale pulls his hand away and lets his sword fall to his side in his right hand. Gwyn thrusts again at Dale's unprotected body, but Dale parries and grits his teeth against the stinging pain.

Gwyn laughs as he moves around Dale, "What fun! You are actually an adequate opponent. I have a hard time deciding...should I cut you into slow bleeding bits or just run you through and be done."

Dale lunges at Gwyn and Gwyn blocks then with quick graceful movement he knocks the sword from Dale's hand sending it to perch at the precipice of the stone wall.

Dale glances past Gwyn at the sword. Again that agonizing smile appears on Gwyn's face. He comes at Dale with thrusts that Dale evades agilely as they move about, but only for a time. Gwyn has been teasing Dale, but now he begins to use his masterful skill. Gwyn gets in close and delivers a couple of good slices on Dale's arm and shoulder.

The pain is intense and Dale glances at his sword. It is so close, yet so far with nothing to block Gwyn's slicing blows. Dale tries to evade Gwyn moving backwards around the pit wall to come up on his sword from the other side, but always Gwyn's dancing balestras keep him on his guard and unable to get closer to it.

The crowd has grown silent in concentration of the fight and so Aslinn's moan as she slips quickly into sleep draws everyone's attention, including Gwyn.

Gwyn glances at her slumped in her chair and Dale takes his advantage and rushes at Gwyn knocking him off his feet and giving Dale the opportunity he needs. He rushes for his sword.

Dale just reaches the sword and grasps it. He turns to find Gwyn is already upon him. Dale blocks Gwyn's strike of blade with blade and the men are pressed close, locked in a struggle of brute strength.

Gwyn pushes his weight and blade tightly against Dale driving him back onto the low wall. Dale can hear the bubbling boiling molten and feel the heat of the fiery pit against his back. The pain of his injuries is intense in his effort to hold Gwyn off and keep from falling back into the pit. Gwyn's eyes burn in his. There is no smirkish smile; hatred and death are etched in Gwyn's face.

Dale thinks of his loving mother, the only one who ever believed in him and he's not sure if his thoughts of love weakens Gwyn or strengthens him, but he feels Gwyn move back just enough to get in a close body blow that sends Gwyn flying backward.

Dale holds onto the wall to steady himself and Gwyn raises his sword and prepares to come at Dale again. "It has been such fun, but I grow weary of you."

Dale chides, "What's the matter Gwyn, can't take it?"

Gwyn lunges and swings the heavy iron sword at Dale's head. Dale ducks. He clings to the wall as he moves around it for Gwyn gives him no chance to advance. His wounds are still searing and weakening him with every movement. Dale brings his sword up to block Gwyn's next swing which comes down on top of Dale's sword with such force that it knocks it loose from his hand again and this time sends it tumbling and clanging against the stone wall into the far recesses of the pit.

The crowd cheers and Dale glances up at Gwyn's smiling face. Gwyn turns slightly to bow to his cheering subjects before delivering the final stroke that will end Dale's life and again Dale is grateful for Gwyn's immense ego. Dale kicks at Gwyn's hand and knocks the sword loose from Gwyn's grip. Gwyn gapes in surprise as he watches it fly across the courtyard.

"It's not so easy to defeat me is it, Gwyn?"

"Look at you." Bloody gashes mark Dale's body, "and still so much faith."

Gwyn demonstrates his strength against Dale's weakened condition and sends Dale flying to the ground with a back arm blow. Before Dale can regain his position Gwyn is upon him again. He throws Dale against the pit wall and glowers, "Can you survive on faith alone?"

Dale staggers and Gwyn strikes him again with such force it sends Dale over the wall. Clinging and dangling, Dale glances at the spewing fire at the bottom of the deep pit and struggles for strength to pull himself up, but his injuries won't support him for long.

Gwyn saunters to his sword, picks it up and faces the crowd. A tear moves down Beth's cheek as Gwyn addresses the crowd. "Who is King?"

The crowd chants: "GWYN! GWYN! GWYN!" and Gwyn takes a deep bow and moves back to the pit.

Dale holds on with his right hand and just manages to get his left elbow up on the wall. He struggles to pull himself up as Gwyn approaches. He hasn't much time and just gets both elbows up when he finds himself staring into Gwyn's evil face.

"Welcome to hell Dale of Glastonbury," and Gwyn raises his sword.

Dale musters all his strength as he swings his body over the wall and tumbles into Gwyn, knocking him off balance. With renewed spirit Dale grabs Gwyn's sword arm and spins him around. He shoves himself against Gwyn and forces him against the wall.

Dale smiles into Gwyn's startled face, "Remember our bargain," and Dale throws Gwyn over the wall. "Now you know who the true King is?"

Gwyn's screams echo through the air as he falls and the crowd goes silent.

Dale feels his wounds begin to heal. He rushes to Beth and pulls her up. The look in her eyes tells him that she understands and he takes the iodine bottle from her hand and begins to uncap it.

Aslinn runs up behind him and jerks Dale around. "I want to know -- did you suffer for having left me here?"

"Every day of my life."

"Then I hope you suffer more for leaving her also."

"We had a bargain. I tried to save you Aslinn, but you gave in too easily. I beg you, help me now -- help her. She's your sister."

Aslinn looks at the bottle Dale holds in his hand, but she throws her head back and laughs. "It's too late for her, just as it was with me. You've won nothing for the result is the same as if you had lost, you go back alone.

Dale grabs her, "Set her free Aslinn -- keep me if you must, but let Beth go!"

Aslinn sneers with hate-filled evil in her eyes. She glances back at the bottle in Dale's hand and snatches it out of his grasp.

Dale pulls her back before she has time to run. He wraps his arm around her and tries to wrestle the bottle out of her hand. Aslinn struggles against him, but keeps both hands clasped tightly around it. Weary and angered by her incessant struggle Dale spins her around, grips her hands and pries on her fingers to pull one hand off the other. He succeeds, but then she uses her free hand to dig her fingernails into his skin and rip the flesh on the back of his hand.

Dale winces in pain, but continues to pull on her fingers clasped around the bottle. There must be a way to save Beth or Aslinn wouldn't be fighting him so hard. With two fingers pried away he can see it now, but Aslinn pulls her hand back and it slips and falls out of her hand. Dale reaches for it, but it's too late and the bottle smashes to the ground at his feet.

A mist rises.

Beth swoons in Dale's arms. It's a cool, starry night. The lights of the town shine in the distance. Beth moans and as the trance lifts so does the haze of fog in her mind.

Dale gazes around in startled disbelief. Beth stares, confused and then they look at each other and their understanding is complete. They wrap their arms around each other exultantly and Dale cries out. "We're home, Beth -- home!"

Beth holds him tight then looks at him and smiles. "You really are King of the Tor."

Dale laughs, swings her around in his arms. "Tonight I'm king of the world."

They spin and laugh against a starry background feeling indeed as if the top of the world is on top of the Tor.

Dale and Beth skipped playfully down the Tor path, laughing and singing as they had when they were children. Their release is so complete; their joy so great that even the thought of the world with all its burdens seems a delightful paradise.

Even the thought of the long walk toward town is a joyous one for their senses are so full of all of life around them in relief to the dry dead environment of Annwn and it becomes like a game as they comment on everything.

Beth stretches her arms and twirls around,
"The air..."

Dale laughs as he watches her, "Crisp and moist it dampens the ground in dew."

Beth laughs, "You sound like a poet."

Dale kicks a stone, "Crickets! Hear them?"

"Hmm. What a beautiful sound."

Dale stops and stares out at the town and Beth stops to see what has alarmed him. "What's wrong?"

Dale smiles, "Nothing. It's a beautiful sight isn't it?"

Beth looks out. Lights flick on and off in town as people go about their business in the early evening. She looks around and sees car lights on the highway in the distance and thinks how they look like signals and beacons to greet them.

Then suddenly they hear rumbling sounds behind them. They turn to see a truck motoring up the road towards them. They wait in the road and Beth waves at the driver of the truck and he pulls up to a stop. Two large dogs in the front seat bark at them and they move to the driver's side.

Beth cries out elatedly, "Mr. MacFadden! Isn't it a lovely night?"

Mr. MacFadden gapes at them. Beth and Dale glance at each other happily then back to Mr. MacFadden's astonished face.

"I said isn't it a lovely --"

Mr. MacFadden turns to his yapping dogs. "Quiet Henry, Jack." Then he turns back to them and blinks, "By Jove it is you!"

Dale steps up close. "What's today's date?"

"You've been missing three months now. The children got back a couple of weeks ago."

Dale and Beth glance at each other.

"We knew it wouldn't be much longer. By Jove I can't believe it. Hop in. Lucy's with Agnes Dewar and Doctor Hall. They'd be at your house about now, lad."

Dale helps Beth into the back of the truck and gets in just as Mr. MacFadden jerks the truck in gear and pulls off down the road.

Not even the hard bumpy ride in the back of Mr. MacFadden's truck is enough to dampen their spirits. Each hard bump sends Beth flying off her bum and back again onto the hard metal bed with an *ouch* of pain and a laugh of silly fun.

Then as they approach the edge of town Mr. MacFadden yells back to them from the cab window. "You got many a believer now lad. People been talkin' nothin' but this since the kiddies got back with their wild tales. We been keepin' watch for yer return ere since."

Dale and Beth smile at each happily. Mr. MacFadden blows his horn and yells out the window as they drive past a few homes at the edge of town. "It's them! They're back. Dale and Beth are back from Annwn."

People stop in their tracks and stare or come outside to see what's going on. Mr. MacFadden continues through town this way, blowing his horn and yelling out that Dale and Beth are back. People wave back and yell out to Dale and Beth and the commotion brings others outside to see what is happening and a crowd of people and cars begins to form behind the truck as they motor slowly through town.

Dale is astonished at the reception. To have the people of Glastonbury actually glad to see him is much more than he ever expected and he's feeling a little confused about it.

Beth is elated with the welcome, not only for her, but especially for Dale. She waves back and it makes her feel like a celebrity in a parade.

People continue to jump into the procession that has formed both in front and behind them now, slowing their progress even farther and the longer it takes the more they both begin to feel the anxiety to get home quickly.

Beth bites her lip, looks at Dale anxiously and cries out. "Three months! Oh, my poor Lucy..."

Dale takes her hand. "He said they'd only been back a few weeks."

"Still..."

Dale nods, his thoughts are of his mother. Three months when she'd been so ill. He knew it more likely that Doctor Hall had been holding vigilantly at his home for their return rather than to expect his mother was still living. Still, he could not help but to hope.

Doctor Hall rests in a chair by the window. The sound of the phone ringing downstairs interrupts his thoughts and he stretches and glances at his watch. The sound of a rush of footsteps coming up the stairs startles him and he sits up attentively. The footsteps are too heavy to be Lucy's and he can't imagine Mrs. Dewar's rather round frame bounding up the stairs in such haste.

His mind immediately determines that there must be some medical emergency and just as he's about to jump to his feet for his medical bag Agnes Dewar runs in the door huffing and panting.

She leans against the door frame, her hand on her heart. Doctor Hall grabs his medical bag ready to run to whatever emergency has arrived then wonders if she won't be the first.

Agnes Dewar gasps a breath, "Doctor Hall!" She pants again, "They're back!"

Doctor Hall stops in mid stride, confused. "What?"

She jumps up and down excitedly and he's sure she's going to need attention if she doesn't calm herself.

"Mrs. Dewar..."

160

"They're back! They're back -- Dale and Beth. They're on their way this minute."

Doctor Hall walks over and takes both her arms in his hands and looks straight into her eyes. "Are you sure?"

Before she can answer the sounds of car horns and cheering voices outside rises in the distance. They run to the window to look out.

The parade of lights from vehicles and people stretches well beyond view and Doctor Hall turns to Agnes Dewar's gleaming, teary face. He grabs her in big hug and kisses her cheek. Then, as if they've both had the same thought they turn a thoughtful gaze on Mrs. Conklin.

She lies still and quiet in her bed. She had been drifting in and out of consciousness for days. Doctor Hall knows that this is what she has been waiting for, but now he wonders if it isn't too late for her to know that at last it has come.

He turns back to Mrs. Dewar. Her lips are pursed in similar contemplation. Then he looks back out at the nearing procession and excitedly he exclaims, "Well -- go put on some tea or something."

"Oh my, oh yes."

Agnes runs out the door and Doctor Hall chuckles, he never would have expected she could move with such speed. He goes to sit beside Mrs. Conklin, takes her hand and whispers, "What a good girl you are to have waited so long. Your wait is almost over now, dear."

He turns back toward the window. The noise of the crowd is increasing and he knows they are almost here.

"You hear that? It's all for him. He's not an outcast in Glastonbury anymore, he's their greatest hero."

Mrs. Dewar fumbles nervously with the teapot, clattering the small ceramic lid into place. Lucy stands on a chair at the kitchen table looking out at the kitchen door window. When Lucy screeches with delight at the sight of Dale and Beth at the door it startles Mrs. Dewar so that she tips a tea cup off its saucer in another scrambling clatter.

The door flings wide open and Beth runs to Lucy and grabs her up off the chair in a big hug.

"Mummy!" Lucy holds tight around her neck and wraps her legs around her.

"Oh, my precious sweet!"

Dale glances at Agnes Dewar who stares teary eyed then runs to him and hugs him. Dale is startled by her abruptness and she holds on while she sobs, "Oh, we're so glad you're back. We've all been praying for you."

She unwraps her plump arms from his neck, steps back and glances down as if embarrassed about her outburst. She wipes her tears and Dale puts his hand on her arm, "Thank you, Mrs. Dewar, I'm sure it helped. Then he pauses, afraid to ask, "My mother?"

She wipes her face and looks up at him sadly. Beth still holds Lucy, but she holds her breath to hear Mrs. Dewar's reply. Dale is sure that she means to deliver the bad news and then she says, "Poor love's been barely holding on just to know you're safe."

Dale's heart leaps with the unexpected news and he starts past her, but she stops him. "She's been...Oh, bother, go to her, Dale, she'll know it's you."

Beth and Mrs. Dewar glance at each other and watch Dale go out of the room.

Doctor Hall rises from the bedside chair as Dale comes in. They glance at each other speechlessly then Dale goes over to her. He kisses her cheek and takes her hand, but there is no response. Overwhelmed with emotion at finding her still here, yet disheartened to see her in this condition, Dale sucks in his breath to hold back tears.

"You are the one person in my life who ever believed in me."

Doctor Hall clears his throat choking on his own emotions, "We all believe in you now, Dale."

Dale's eyes close in anguish, but then he feels a slight squeeze of his hand and he opens them. His mother's eyes flutter, open then at last they find him and she smiles.

Dale chokes on his words, fighting back tears. "So how many dates have you two been on? Do I have anything to worry about?"

She gazes at him with a glint in her eyes that speaks volumes of love although her smile is weak. Her voice is weak too. "What took...so long?"

Dale's emotion finally overcomes him and he wipes a tear. "It's barely been a day. Did you miss me?"

Her smile broadens and her eyes close briefly and she whispers.

"Just wanted to know you were all right...don't have to worry about you..."

"You don't have to worry about me anymore."

Her eyes open wide, she looks at Dale. "So proud...always been so proud of you."

Her eyes close.

"I love you mother."

"My prayers have been answered...I always knew you were special."

Her breath slows. Dale holds her hand and the tears flow as he watches her draw her last breath.

He gasps tearful breathes as he tries to control his tears then kisses her cheek and still holding her hand he gazes at her.

Doctor Hall squeezes Dale's shoulder and wipes at the tear that slides down his cheek.

Lucy runs around the yard and squeals happily at the puppy chasing her heels.

Beth turns to Dale. "Really, Dale -- a puppy, don't you think you could have asked me first?"

"Of course not, you might have said no."

They break into laughter then turn to the sound of an approaching automobile. Doctor Hall waves as he drives up. Lucy waves back at him and picks up the puppy to show to him. The puppy squirms in her arms and flops down on the ground and she chases the puppy as it wobbles around.

Doctor Hall walks up to Dale and Beth.

"New puppy?"

Beth shoots a sharp look at Dale, "Wasn't my idea."

The men grasp hands. "Good to see you, David."

They stand and watch Lucy with the puppy and Doctor Hall says, "Glad to hear you've decided to stay on a bit." He glances between Dale and Beth knowingly and Dale grins.

"Glastonbury's become home to me again."

"Well they do say home is where the heart is. Will I see you at the celebration tonight?"

Dale shakes his head. "We've been through a lot -- and I don't mean to appear ungrateful, but I don't really care for being called King of the Tor anymore."

Beth takes Dale's hand and smiles up at him. "Then how do you feel about being king of my world?"

"Now there's a position I'd happily take."

Dale picks Beth up in his arms and swings her around in a happy hug. Doctor Hall gleams and thinks to himself, *Now that's what I like, a happy ending.*

A light breeze floats a leaf through the air and beyond it the Tor stands like a beacon against the surrounding lowland.

THE END

www.ingramcontent.com/pod-product-compliance
Lightning Source LLC
Chambersburg PA
CBHW070924130626
46555CB00001B/273